The Vineyards of Calanetti
Saying "I do" under the Tuscan sun...

Deep in the Tuscan countryside nestles
the picturesque village of Monte Calanetti.
Famed for its world-renowned vineyards, the
village is also home to the crumbling but beautiful
Palazzo di Comparino. Empty for months, rumors of
a new owner are spreading like wildfire...and that's
before the village is chosen as the setting for the
royal wedding of the year!

It's going to be a roller coaster of a year, but will
wedding bells ring out in Monte Calanetti for
anyone else?

Find out in this fabulously heartwarming, uplifting
and thrillingly romantic new eight-book continuity
from Harlequin Romance!

Dear Reader,

Oh, what fun it's been to travel to Tuscany! Not for real, though someday I'd love to go. But that's one of the best things about reading, the travel to faraway places all done from the comfort of our armchairs, beds, sun lounges. I have to give a shout-out to all my fellow authors in the series. Hey, ladies! What fun to work with these talented, dedicated authors. The editors gave us a good start, but the emails flew back and forth as we mapped it out, created the plaza and the fountain and filled the cheerful town with people.

A special thanks to Rebecca Winters, whose book follows mine. She had great patience with me as I planned her character's wedding. I sent her pictures of wedding dresses, tiaras and reception pictures. With her permission I used some beautiful words from her wedding ceremony during the rehearsal. I won't say anything more or I might spoil something for you. Happy reading.

Ciao!

Teresa Carpenter

The Best Man & The Wedding Planner

Teresa Carpenter

—

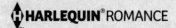

Recycling programs for this product may not exist in your area.

Special thanks and acknowledgment are given to Teresa Carpenter for her contribution to The Vineyards of Calanetti series.

ISBN-13: 978-0-373-74364-3

The Best Man & The Wedding Planner

First North American Publication 2015

Copyright © 2015 by Harlequin Books S.A.

HARLEQUIN®
™ www.Harlequin.com

Printed in U.S.A.

Teresa Carpenter believes that with love and family anything is possible. She writes in a Southern California coastal city surrounded by her large family. Teresa loves writing about babies and grandmas. Her books have rated as Top Picks by *RT Book Reviews* and have been nominated Best Romance of the Year on some review sites. If she's not at a family event, she's reading or writing her next grand romance.

Books by Teresa Carpenter

Harlequin Romance

The Sheriff's Doorstep Baby
The Making of a Princess
Stolen Kiss From a Prince
Her Boss by Arrangement
A Pregnancy, a Party & a Proposal
His Unforgettable Fiancée

Visit the Author Profile page
at Harlequin.com for more titles.

This book is dedicated to my editor
Carly Byrne for her patience, understanding,
speed and good cheer. I never see her sweat.
Even when I do. Thank you for everything.

CHAPTER ONE

"Now boarding, first-class passengers for Flight 510 to Florence."

Lindsay Reeves's ears perked up. She glanced at her watch; time had gotten away from her. She closed her tablet folio, tucked it into her satchel and then reached for the precious cargo she was personally escorting across the ocean. She hooked the garment bag holding the couture wedding dress for the future Queen of Halencia over her shoulder and began to move as the attendant made a second announcement. "First-class passengers now boarding."

"Welcome aboard." The attendant looked from the second ticket to Lindsay. "I'm sorry, both passengers will need to be present to board."

"We're both here. I bought a seat for this." She held up the garment bag.

The woman smiled but her eyes questioned Lindsay's sanity. "You bought a first-class ticket for your luggage?"

"Yes." She kept it at that, not wanting to draw any

further attention. With the wedding only a month away, the world was alive with wedding dress fever.

"We have a storage closet in first class that can hold it if you want to refund the ticket before take-off," the attendant offered.

"No, thank you." Lindsay pressed the second ticket into the woman's hand. "I'm not letting this bag out of my sight."

On the plane she passed a nice-looking older couple already seated in the first row and moved on to the last row where she spied her seats. She draped the garment bag over the aisle seat and frowned when it immediately slumped into a scrunched heap on the seat.

That wouldn't do. She pulled it back into place and tried to anchor it but when she let go, it drooped again. The weight of the dress, easily thirty pounds, made it too heavy to lie nicely. She needed something to hold it in place. After using her satchel to counter the weight temporarily, she slid past a young couple and their two children to speak to the flight attendant.

"We have a closet we can hang the dress in," the male attendant stated upon hearing her request.

"I've been paid not to let it out of my sight," she responded. True enough. Her reputation as a wedding planner to the rich and famous depended on her getting this dress to the wedding in pristine condition without anyone seeing it but her, the bride and her attendants.

"Hmm," the man—his name tag read Dan—tapped his lips while he thought.

"Welcome aboard, sir." Behind Lindsay another attendant, a blonde woman, greeted a fellow passenger.

Out of the corner of her eye Lindsay got the impression of a very tall, very broad, dark-haired man. She stepped into the galley to give them more room.

"You're the last of our first-class passengers," the attendant advised the man. "Once you're seated, please let me know if you need anything."

"Check," the man said in a deep, bass voice and moved down the aisle.

Goodness. Just the one word sent a tingle down Lindsay's spine. She sure hoped he intended to sleep during the long, red-eye flight. She wanted to get some work done and his voice might prove quite distracting.

"I've got it." Dan waved a triumphant hand. "We'll just put the seat in sleep mode and lay the bag across it." He poured a glass of champagne and then another. "Will that work?"

"Yes, that will be perfect. Thank you."

"Seats aren't allowed to be reclined during takeoff. Once we reach cruising altitude I'll be along to put the seat down. And I'll look for something to secure it in case the flight gets bumpy."

"Great. You've been very helpful."

Lindsay headed back to her seat. Halfway through first class she caught sight of the newcomer and her breath caught in the back of her throat. He was beautiful. There was no other word for it. Long, lean features with high cheekbones, dark, slanted eyebrows and long, black eyelashes. Dark stubble decorated his square jaw.

Suddenly her eyes popped wide and she let out a shriek. "Get up!" she demanded. "Get up right now!"

He was sitting on the dress!

A frown furrowed his brow. He slowly opened lambent brown eyes so stunning she almost forgot why she was yelling. Almost.

"Are you talking to me?" he asked in a deep, rasping voice.

"Yes." She confronted the man, hands on hips. "You're in my seat. Sitting on my dress. Get up!"

"What's the problem here?" The other attendant appeared next to her.

"He's in my seat." She pointed an accusing finger. "Sitting on my garment bag. Make him move."

Behind her a young child began to cry. Lindsay cringed but held her ground.

The beading on this dress was intricate, all hand-sewn. If it had to be repaired it would cost a fortune. And she'd already paid a pretty penny to make sure nothing happened to it. How could someone sit on a garment bag without noticing it?

"Let's all calm down." The blonde attendant squeezed by Lindsay. "Sir, can I ask you to stand, please?"

The man slowly rose. He had to duck to the side to avoid hitting the overhead compartment. He must be six-four, maybe six-five; a long way to glare up from five feet four. She managed.

"I'm not sitting on anything." He gestured across the aisle. "I moved it there because it was in my seat."

Lindsay looked to her left. The garment bag rested in a heap on the seat with her heavy satchel dumped on top. She jumped on it, removing her bag and smoothing the fabric. It was all mushed as though it had been sat on.

"May I see your tickets, please?" Dan requested.

Lindsay pulled hers from the front pocket of her satchel and waited to be vindicated.

"Actually, you're both in wrong seats. My fault, I'm afraid. I'm used to a different plane. I do apologize. Ms. Reeves, you are on the left and, Mr. Sullivan, you need to move forward a row."

Lovely. She couldn't even blame the beast. Except she did.

At least he'd be in the row ahead of her so she wouldn't have to have him next to her the entire flight.

His brown gaze went to the toddlers in the row in front of the one the attendant indicated. "I'd prefer the back row." He pasted on a charming smile. "Is it possible to trade seats?"

No. No. No.

"Of course." The blonde gushed, swayed, no doubt, by his dimples. "There was a cancellation so no one else is boarding in first class. Is there anything I can get you before we continue boarding?"

"A pillow would be nice."

"My pleasure, Mr. Sullivan." She turned to Lindsay. "Anything for you, ma'am?"

Ma'am? Seriously? "I'd like a pillow. And a blanket, please."

"We'll do a full turndown service after the flight gets started." She gave Sullivan a smile and disappeared behind the curtain to the coach area.

Lindsay stared after her. Did that mean she didn't get a pillow or a blanket? This was her first time flying first-class. So far she had mixed feelings. She liked the extra room and the thought of stretching out for the long flight. But Blondie wasn't earning any points.

Lindsay draped the garment bag over the window seat as best she could until the seat could be reclined. Unfortunately that put her in the aisle seat directly across from Mr. Tall, Dark and Inconsiderate.

Nothing for it. She'd just have to ignore him and

focus on her work. It would take the entire flight to configure the seating arrangement for the reception. She had the list of guests from the bride and the list of guests from the groom. And a three-page list of political notes from the palace of who couldn't be seated next to whom and who should be seated closer to the royal couple. What had started as a private country wedding had grown to include more than a hundred guests as political factors came into play.

It was a wedding planner's nightmare. But she took it as an opportunity to excel.

Before she knew it she was being pushed back in her chair as the plane lifted into the air. Soon after, Dan appeared to fold down the window seat. He carefully laid the heavy garment bag in place and secured it with the seat belt and a bungee cord. She thanked him as she resumed her seat.

She glanced out of the corner of her eye to see Sullivan had his pillow—a nice, big, fluffy one. Ignore him. Easier thought than done. He smelled great; a spicy musk with a touch of soap.

Eyes back on her tablet, she shuffled some names into table seats and then started to run them against her lists to see if they were all compatible. Of course, they weren't. Two people needed to be moved forward and two people couldn't be seated together. That left four people at the table. She moved people to new tables and highlighted them as a reminder to check out the politics on them. And repeated the process.

A soft snore came from across the way—much less annoying than the shrill cry of one of the toddlers demanding a bandage for his boo-boo. Blondie rushed to the rescue and the boy settled down. Except for loud outbursts like that, the two boys were actually well behaved. There'd been no need for Sullivan to move seats.

"Would you care for a meal, Ms. Reeves?" Dan appeared beside her.

She glanced at the time on her tablet. Eight o'clock. They'd been in the air an hour. "Yes, please."

"You have a choice of chicken Cordon bleu or beef Stroganoff."

"I'll have the beef. With a cola."

He nodded and turned to the other side of the aisle. Before he could ask, Sullivan said he'd have the beef and water.

Her gaze collided with his. Brown eyes with specks of gold surveyed her, interest and appreciation sparkled in the whiskey-brown depths, warm and potent.

Heat flooded her, followed by a shiver.

"What's in the bag?" he asked, his voice even deeper and raspier from sleep. Way too sexy for her peace of mind.

"None of your business." She turned back to her table plan.

"Must be pretty important for you to get so upset. Let me guess, a special dress for a special occasion?" He didn't give up.

"Yes. If you must know. And it's my job to protect it."

"Protect it? Interesting. So it's not your dress."

She rolled her eyes and sent him a droll stare. "I liked you better when you were snoring."

He grinned, making his dimples pop. "I deserve that. Listen, I'm sorry for my attitude earlier and for sitting on the dress. I had wine with dinner and wine always gives me a headache."

Lindsay glared at Sullivan. "So you did sit on the dress." She knew it. That had definitely been a butt print on the bag.

He blinked, all innocence. "I meant I'm sorry for dumping it over there."

"Uh-huh."

His grin never wavered.

"Why did you have wine with dinner if it gives you a headache?"

The smile faded. "Because dinner with my folks always goes better with a little wine. And I'm going to have a headache at the end either way."

"Okay, I get that." Lindsay adored her flighty, dependent mother but, yeah, dinners were easier with a little wine. Sometimes, like between husbands, a lot of wine was required.

A corner of his rather nice mouth kicked up. "You

surprise me, Ms. Reeves. I'd have thought you'd be appalled."

"Parents aren't always easy." She closed her tablet to get ready for her meal. "It doesn't mean we don't love them."

"Amen. Respect is another matter."

That brought her attention around. He wore a grim expression and turmoil churned in his distracted gaze. The situation with his parents must be complicated. It was a sad day when you lost respect for the person you loved most in the world. She understood his pain only too well.

Thankfully, Dan arrived with a small cart, disrupting old memories. He activated a tray on the side of her seat and placed a covered plate in front of her along with a glass of soda. Real china, real crystal, real silverware. Nice. And then he lifted the cover and the luscious scent of braised meat and rich sauce reached her.

"Mmm." She hummed her approval. "This looks fantastic."

"I can promise you it is," Dan assured her. "Chef LaSalle is the pride of the skies."

She took her first bite as he served Sullivan and moaned again. She couldn't help it, the flavors burst in her mouth, seducing her taste buds.

"Careful, Ms. Reeves," Sullivan cautioned. "You sound like you're having a good time over there."

"Eat. You'll understand." She took a sip of her

drink, watching him take a bite. "Or maybe not. After all, you've already eaten."

"I wasn't hungry earlier. Damn, this is good." He pointed to the video screen. "Shall we watch a movie with our meal?"

She was tempted. Surprising. After the disaster of last year, work had been her major consolation. She rarely took the time to relax with a movie. She was too busy handling events for the stars of those movies. A girl had to work hard to make the stars happy in Hollywood. And she had to work harder than the rest after allowing an old flame to distract her to the point of putting her career at risk. But she'd learned her lesson.

Luckily she'd already signed the contract for this gig. And she planned to make the royal wedding of the Crown Prince of Halencia, Antonio de l'Accardi, to the commoner, Christina Rose, the wedding of the century.

Thirty days from now no one would be able to question her dedication—which meant returning to the puzzle of the table seating.

"You go on," she told Sullivan. "I have to get back to my work."

"What are you doing over there? Those earlier moans weren't as pleasant as your dinner noises."

"It's a creative new form of torture called a seating arrangement."

"Ah. It sounds excruciating."

"Oh, believe me. It's for a political dinner and there are all these levels of protocols of who can sit with whom. And then there's the added element of personal likes and dislikes. It's two steps back for every one step forward. And it's a lot of manual double-checking…talk about a headache."

"Politics usually are." The grimness in his tone told her there was something more there. Before she had time to wonder about it, he went on. "The information isn't on spreadsheets?"

"It is, but there are more than a hundred names here. I have to seat a table and then check each name to see if they're compatible."

"You know you can set up a program that can look at the information and tell you whether the table mates are compatible at the time you put the name in."

She blinked at him. "That would be wonderful. How do I do that exactly?"

He laughed, a deep, friendly sound, then rattled off a string of commands that had her eyes glazing over. "The setup will take a few minutes but will likely save you hours overall."

"Yeah, but you lost me at the word 'algorithm.'" She wiped her mouth with the cloth napkin. "You really had my hopes up for a minute there."

"Sorry, tech talk. I own a company that provides software for cyber security. A program like this really isn't that difficult. Let me see your computer after dinner and I'll do it for you. It'll take me less than an hour."

This man was tempting her left and right. She weighed the hours she'd save against the confidentiality agreement she'd signed and sadly shook her head.

"Thank you for offering but I can't. This is a special event. I'm not allowed to share information with anyone except my staff, designated officials and pre-approved vendors."

"This is for the royal wedding of Prince Antonio of Halencia, right?"

Her eyes popped wide. How could he know that?

"Come on, it's not hard to guess. The wedding dress, the seating chart. We're on a flight to Florence. And I know they have an American event planner. Hang on, I'll take care of this."

He pulled out his cell phone and hit a couple of buttons.

"What?" she challenged. "You're calling the palace in Halencia? Uh, huh. I don't think so. You can hang up now."

"Hey, Tony." He raised a dark eyebrow as he spoke into the phone.

Tony? As in Antonio? Yeah, right.

"I got your text. Don't worry about it. I'm here for a month. I'll see you next week." He listened for a moment. "Yes, I had dinner with them. They were thrilled with the invitation. Hey, listen, the wedding

planner is on my flight and she needs some pro-
gramming to help her with the seating chart. She's
bound by the confidentiality agreement from letting me help her. Can you give her authorization?
Great, I'm going to put her on."

He held the phone out to Lindsay. "It's Prince
Antonio."

CHAPTER TWO

LINDSAY ROLLED HER eyes at the man across the way, wondering how far he meant to take this joke and what he hoped to achieve.

"Hello?"

"*Buona sera*, Ms. Reeves. I hope you are having a nice flight."

"Uh, yes, I am." The voice was male, pleasant and slightly accented. And could be anyone. Except how had he known her name? Sullivan hadn't mentioned it.

"Christina is thrilled to have your services for the wedding. You have my full support to make this *il matrimonio dei suoi sogni*—the wedding of her dreams."

"I'll do my best." Could this actually be the prince?

"Duty demands my presence at the palace but I look forward to meeting you at the rehearsal. Zach is my best man. He will be my advocate in Monte Calanetti for the next month. He is available to assist you in any way necessary."

She turned to look at the man across the aisle and quirked a brow at his evil smirk. "Zach… Sullivan?"

"Yes. We went to college together. He's like a brother to me. If he can assist with the meal plan—"

"The seating chart." She squeezed her eyes closed. *OMG, I just interrupted the royal prince.*

"Of course. The seating chart. If Zach can help, you must allow him to be of service. He is quite handy with a computer."

"Yes. I will. Thank you."

"It is I who thanks you. You do us an honor by coming to Halencia. If I can be of further assistance, you have access to me through Zach. *Buona notte*, Ms. Reeves."

"Good night." Instead of giving the phone back to Sullivan she checked the call history and saw she'd spoken to Tony de l'Accardi. She slowly turned her head to meet chocolate-brown eyes. "You know the Prince of Halencia."

"I wouldn't take on the best man gig for anyone else."

The flight attendant appeared with the cart to collect his meal and sweetly inquire if he'd like dessert.

Lindsay rolled her eyes, barely completing the action before the blonde turned to her.

"Are you done, ma'am?"

Ma'am again? Lindsay's eyes narrowed in a bland stare.

Her displeasure must have registered because the woman rushed on. "For dessert we have crème brûlée, strawberry cheesecake or a chocolate mousse."

Lindsay handed off her empty plate and, looking the woman straight in the eye, declared, "I'll have one of each."

"Of course, ma... Ms. Reeves." She hurriedly stashed the plate and rolled the cart away.

Lindsay slowly turned her head until Sullivan's intent regard came into view. Okay, first things first. "I'm only twenty-nine. Way too young to be ma'am."

He cocked his head.

She handed him his phone. "Why didn't you tell me you were the best man?"

He lifted one dark eyebrow. "Would you have believed me?"

She contemplated him. "Probably. I have a file on you."

His slanted eyebrow seemed to dip even further. "Then I'm surprised you didn't recognize me. You probably have profiles on the entire wedding party in that tablet of yours."

She lifted one shoulder in a half shrug of acknowledgment. "I've learned it's wise to know who I'll be working with. I didn't recognize you because it's out of context. Plus, you don't have an eight-o'clock shadow in your company photo in which you're wearing glasses."

"Huh." He ran the backs of his fingers over his jaw. "I'll have to get that picture updated. I had Lasik eye surgery over a year ago. Regardless, I didn't know you were involved in the wedding until you started talking about the meal arrangements."

"Seating arrangements," she corrected automatically.

"Right."

The flight attendant arrived with dessert. She handed Zach a crystal dish of chocolate mousse and set a small tray with all three desserts artfully displayed in front of Lindsay.

"Enjoy," she said and retreated down the aisle.

"Mmm." Lindsay picked up a spoon and broke into the hard shell of crystalized sugar topping the crème brûlée. "Mmm." This time it was a moan. "Oh, that's good."

"Careful, Ms. Reeves, you're going to get me worked up if you continue." Zach gestured at her loaded tray with his spoon. "I see you like your sweets."

"It's a long night." She defended her stash.

"I guess you don't plan on sleeping."

"I have a lot of work." She gave her usual excuse then, for some unknown reason, confessed, "I don't sleep well on planes."

"It may help if you relaxed and watched the movie instead of working."

No doubt he was right. But work soothed her, usually. Over the past year she'd found it increasingly more difficult to believe in the magic of her process. She blamed her breakup with Kevin last year. But she hoped to change that soon. If a royal wedding couldn't bring back the magic in what she did, she needed to rethink her career path.

"Thank you for that insightful bit of advice. What don't you like about being best man? The role or the exposure?"

"Either. Both. Seems like I've been dodging the limelight since I was two."

"Well, you did grow up in a political family." That brought his earlier comment and reaction into context. Her research revealed he was related to the political powerhouse Sullivans from Connecticut. "Never had any aspiration in that direction?"

The curse he uttered made her glance worriedly toward the toddlers. Luckily the lack of sound or movement in that direction indicated they were probably asleep.

"I'll take that as a no."

"I wished my father understood me so well."

She empathized with his pain. She felt the same way about her mother. Perhaps empathy was why she found him so easy to talk to. "I've found parents often see what they want to see. That addresses the exposure…what do you have against the role of best man?"

"I hate weddings. The fancier the event, the more I detest them. There's something about the pomp and circumstance that just screams fake to me." He licked his spoon and set the crystal dish aside. "No offense."

No offense? He'd just slammed everything she stood for. Why should she be offended?

And he wasn't done. "It's like the couple needs to distract the crowd from the fact they're marrying for something other than love."

"You don't believe in love?" It was one thing for her to question her belief in what she was doing and another for someone else to take shots at it.

"I believe in lust and companionship. Love is a myth best left to romance novels."

"Wow. That's harsh." And came way too close to how she felt these days.

The way his features hardened when he voiced his feelings told her strong emotion backed his comment. Kind of at odds with his family dynamic. The Sullivans were touted as one of the All-American families going back for generations. Long marriages and one or two kids who were all upstanding citizens. They ranked right up there with the Kennedys and Rockefellers.

The attendants came through the cabin collecting trash and dirty dishes. They offered turndown service, which Lindsay turned down. She still had work to do.

"Just let us know when you're ready."

Across the way Zach also delayed his bed service and got the same response. Once the attendants moved on, he leaned her way.

"Now you know you can trust me, are you ready for me to work on your spreadsheet? I'd like to do it before I start my movie."

"Oh. Sure." Could she trust him? Lindsay wondered as she pulled out her tablet. Just because she knew who he was didn't mean he was trustworthy. Too charming for her peace of mind. And a total flirt. "Do you want to do it on mine or should I send it to you?"

"Little Pixie, I'd like to do yours." His gaze ran over her, growing hotter as it rolled up her body. Her blood was steaming by the time his gaze met hers. "But since I have to work, you should send it to me."

"It'll do you no good to flirt with me." She tapped in her password and opened her spreadsheet. "What's your email?" She keyed in the address and sent it. "This wedding is too important to my career for me to risk getting involved with the best man."

"Oh, come on. The best man is harmless." Zach had his laptop open. "Got it. He's shackled for the whole event."

"The best man is a beast. His mind is all wrapped up in the bachelor party and strippers. He feels it's his duty to show the groom what he'll be giving up. And more than half the time he's on the prowl for some action just to remind himself he's still free, whether he is or not."

Zach flinched. "Wow. That's harsh."

Oh, clever man. "With good cause. I have a strict 'no fraternizing with the wedding party—including guests'—policy for my company and the vendors I work with. But, yeah, I've had to bolster a few bridesmaids who took it too far and expected too much and went home alone. Or refer them back to the bride or groom for contact info that wasn't shared."

"That's a lot of blame heaped on the best man."

"Of course, it's not just the best man, but in my experience he can be a bad, bad boy."

"It's been a long time since I was bad."

"Define long."

He laughed.

"Seriously, I just want you to rewind the conversation a few sentences and then say that again with a straight face."

His gaze shifted from his laptop to make another slow stroll over her. Jacking up her pulse yet again.

He needed to stop doing that!

Unremorseful, he cocked an eyebrow. "I'm not saying I don't go after what I want. But I'm always up front about my intentions. No illusions, no damages."

Sounded like a bad boy to her.

"Well, you have fun, now. I'm here to work."

He shook his head as he went back to keying commands into his computer. "All work and no play makes Ms. Reeves a dull girl."

"I'm not being paid to have fun." And that was the problem right there—the one she'd been struggling with for nearly a year.

Her work wasn't fun anymore.

And the cause wasn't just the disillusionment she suffered in her love life. Though that ranked high on the motive list. She'd started feeling this way before Kevin had come back into her life. Instead of being excited by the creative endeavor, she'd gotten bogged down in the details.

Maybe it was Hollywood. Believing in the magic of happily-ever-after got a little harder to do with each repeat customer. Not to mention the three-peats. And the fact her mother was her best customer. Hopefully, husband number six would be the charm for her.

Seriously, Lindsay crossed her fingers in the folds of her skirt. She truly wished this marriage lasted. She liked Matt and he seemed to get her mom, who had the attention span and sense of responsibility of a fourteen-year-old. There was nothing mentally wrong with Darlene Reeves. She could do for herself. She just didn't want to. Darlene's dad had treated her like a princess, giving her most everything she wanted and taking care of all the little details in life. He'd died when she was seventeen and she'd been chasing his replacement all her life.

She'd had Lindsay when she was eighteen and then she learned to get the wedding ring on her finger before they lost interest. In between love interests, Lindsay was expected to pick up the slack.

She loved her mother dearly. But she loved her a little easier when she was in a committed relationship.

"Did you fall asleep on me over there?"

His question called her attention to his profile. Such strong features—square jaw dusted with stubble-defined cheekbones, straight nose. He really was beautiful in a totally masculine way. Too much temptation. Good thing her policy put him off limits.

"No. Just going over what I need to do."

"Perfect timing then." He swirled his finger and hit a single key. "Because I just sent your file back to you."

"So soon?" She reached for her tablet, excited to try the new program. The file opened onto a picture of circles in the form of a rectangle. Each circle was numbered. She'd refine the shape once she viewed the venue. She ran her finger across the page and as it moved over a circle names popped up showing who was seated at the table.

"Cool. How do I see everybody?"

"You hit this icon here." He hung over his chair, reaching across the aisle to show her. He tried showing her the other features, but his actions were awkward. Being left-handed, he had to use his right hand to aid her because of the distance between the seats.

"This is ridiculous." Unsnapping her seat belt, she stood. "Do you mind if I come over there for a few minutes while we go over this?"

"Sure." He stood, as well, and stepped aside.

Standing next to him she came face to loosened tie with him. She bent her head back to see him and then bent it back again to meet his gaze. "My goodness. How tall are you?"

"Six-four."

"And the prince?"

"Six-one." Long fingers tugged on a short dark tendril. "Does this brain never stop working?"

"Not when I get a visual of a tall drink of water standing next to a shot glass."

"I'm not quite sure what that means, but I think there was a compliment in there somewhere."

"Don't start imagining things at fifty thousand feet, Sullivan. We're a long way from help." She tugged on his blue-pinstriped tie. "You can ditch this now. Was dinner a formal affair?"

The light went out of his eyes. He yanked the tie off and stuffed it in his pants' pocket. "It's always formal with my parents."

She patted his chest. "You did your duty, now move on."

"Good advice." He gestured for her to take the window seat.

She hesitated for a beat. Being trapped in the inside seat, surrounded by his potent masculinity, might be pushing her self-control a little thin. But his computer program blew her mind. From the tiny bit she'd seen, it had the potential to save her hours, if not days, of work.

"Ms. Reeves?" His breath wafted over her ear, sending a shiver racing down her spine. "Are you okay?"

"Of course." She realized he'd been talking while she fought off her panic attack. "Ah...hmm." She cleared her throat to give herself a moment to calm down. "Why do you keep calling me by my last name?"

"Because I don't know your first name," he stated simply.

Oh, right. The flight attendants had used their last names. The prince had given her Zach's name and then she'd read it on her spreadsheet.

"It's Lindsay."

A slow grin formed, crinkling the corners of his eyes. "Pretty. A pretty name for a pretty girl."

So obvious, yet the words still gave her a bit of a thrill. She pressed her lips together to hide her reaction. "You can't help yourself, can you?"

"What?" All innocence.

"Please. That line is so old I think I heard it in kindergarten."

She expected to see his dimple flash but got an intent stare instead. "It's not a line when it's true."

A little thrill chased goose bumps across her skin. Oh, my, he was good.

She almost believed him.

Shaking her head at him, at herself, she slid past him and dropped into the window seat.

He slid into his seat, his big body filling up the small space. Thankfully they were in first class and a ten-inch console separated their seats, giving her some breathing space. Until he flicked some buttons and the console dropped down.

"That's better."

For who? She leaned away as he leaned closer. Just as she feared, she felt pinned in, crowded. When he dropped the tray down in front of her, the sense of being squeezed from all sides grew stronger. Not by claustrophobia but by awareness. His scent—man and chocolate—made her mouth water.

"So is it easy for you?" He half laughed, going back to their previous conversation. "To move on?"

"It's not, actually. My mom problems are probably just as bad as or worse than your parent problems. Yet, here I am, jetting off to Italy."

Mom's words, not hers. Darlene couldn't understand how Lindsay could leave and be gone for a month when Darlene's next wedding was fast approaching. It didn't matter that Lindsay had booked this event well before Darlene got engaged or that it was the wedding of the year—perhaps the decade—and a huge honor for Lindsay to be asked to handle it.

"I doubt it."

"Really? My mother is my best customer."

"Oh-hh." He dragged the word out.

"Exactly. Soon I'll be walking her down the aisle to husband number six."

"Ouch. Is she a glutton for punishment?"

"Quite the opposite. My mother loves to be in love. The minute a marriage becomes work, it's the beginning of the end. What I can't get her to understand is that you have to work on your marriage from day one. Love needs to be fostered and nourished through respect and compromise."

"Honesty, communication and loyalty are key."

"Yes!" She nudged him in the arm. "You get it. Maybe you won't be such a bad best man, after all."

He lifted one dark eyebrow. "Thanks."

"Anyway. I can waste a lot of time worrying about Mom or I can accept that it's her life to live. Just as my life is mine to live." She didn't know why she was sharing this with him. Her mother's love life wasn't a secret. Far from it. But Lindsay rarely talked about her mother. "Until the next time she comes crying on my shoulder, I choose the latter."

"At least she lets her suckers off the line."

"What does that mean?"

"Nothing." He ran a hand around the back of his neck, loosening tight muscles. "It's hard to let my parents just be when they keep harping on me to join the campaign trail."

"They want you to run for office?"

"Oh, yeah. I'm to stop messing around with my little hobby and turn my mind to upholding the family name by running for the next open seat in congress."

"Hobby? Didn't I read an article that your company just landed a hundred-million-dollar government contract to upgrade electronic security for the military?"

"You did." While he talked he opened the seating arrangement program. "And between that contract and Antonio selling me his share of the business, I've met a goal I set the day I opened my business."

Clearly, resignation overshadowed pride, so she ventured, "You exceeded your father's net worth?"

He shifted to study her. "So you're psychic as well as a wedding planner?"

"When you work with people as closely as I do, you get to know how they think."

"Hmm."

"It's an impressive accomplishment."

The Sullivans came from old money made from banking and transportation. Their political dynasty went back several generations. "Your parents must be proud of you."

"They didn't even mention it. Too focused on when I'd leave it all behind and fall in line with my family obligations." He tapped a few keys and her seating arrangement popped up on the screen. "Feels kind of hollow now."

"I'm sorry."

He didn't look up. "It doesn't matter."

"You mean it didn't matter to them."

He gave a negligent shrug. "I'm a big boy. I can handle it."

"Well, I officially call the parent battle a draw. I know it's not the same but...congratulations."

That earned her a half smile and a nod. Then he started to run her through the features of the computer program.

"This is fabulous." All she had to do was type a name into a seat slot and all the notes associated with that name appeared sorted by category and importance. "You have saved me hours of work."

His eyes gleamed as he went on to show her a few additional options. "And if you do this—" he punched a couple of keys "—it will auto-fill based on a selected category." He clicked social standing and then pressed Enter. Names popped into assigned seats.

She blinked. "Wow. What do the colors mean?" Many of the names were in red and blue.

"Blue means there's a conflict with someone else at the table. Red means there are two or more conflicts."

While he showed her how to access the conflicts, she impulsively pressed the button to call the attendant. The blonde appeared with impressive speed, her smile dimming slightly when she saw Lindsay seated with Zach.

"How can I help you?"

"We'd like two glasses of champagne, please. And some strawberries if you have them."

"I think I can find some. Be right back."

"Champagne?" He cocked his head. "You turned it down earlier."

"That was before. Now we have things to celebrate. I have this to help me finish my seating plan and you met a career-long goal."

The attendant arrived with a tray, setting it down between them. "*Buon appetito!* Ms. Reeves, would you like us to do your turndown service now?"

"Sure." Maybe the champagne would help her sleep. The woman turned away and Lindsay lifted a flute of bubbling gold wine. "To you. Congratulations and thank you."

Zach lifted his flute and tapped it against Lindsay's. "To you." A crystal chime rang out as pretty as the sound of her laughter. Her simple gesture almost undid the butcher job his parent's self-absorption had done to his pride. He didn't get them, probably never would. They couldn't spare the smallest show of affection. But this prickly little pixie put her animosity aside to toast his success.

She didn't know him except as a helpful jerk and a few dry facts on paper. Heck, she hugged the window in an attempt to maintain her distance yet she still celebrated his accomplishment.

It almost made him feel bad about sabotaging the wedding.

CHAPTER THREE

IT WAS A drastic plan. One Zach took no pleasure in. But he'd do whatever necessary to ensure his friend didn't suffer the frigid existence his parents called marriage. Antonio was already sacrificing his life for his country; selling off his business interests in America to Zach. He shouldn't have to give up all chance of happiness, too.

Zach reluctantly agreed to be best man. He didn't believe in big, lavish weddings. And he didn't approve of Tony's insane sacrifice. So why would he agree? Because Tony was the closest thing he had to a brother. Of course, he had to support him.

And of course he felt compelled to talk him out of throwing his future away.

Zach knew the circumstances of Antonio's marriage and it made him sick to think of his honorable, big-hearted friend locked into a miserable existence like his parents had shared.

He wasn't thinking of doing anything overt. Certainly nothing that would embarrass the royal family, especially his best friend. But he could cause a few delays. And earn enough time to talk his friend out of making the biggest mistake of his life.

Tony had a lot on his plate taking on the leadership of his country. Halencia had reached a state of crisis. Antonio's parents were gregarious, bigger-than-life characters madly in love with each other one moment and viciously in hate the next. There'd been public affairs and passionate reconciliations.

The country languished under their inattention. The king and queen lived big and spent big, costing the country much-needed funds.

The citizens of Halencia loved the drama, hated the politics. Demands for a change had started years ago but had become more persistent in the past five years. Until a year ago when the king was threatened with a paternity suit. It turned out Antonio wasn't getting a new sibling. It was just a scare tactic gone wrong.

But it was the last straw for the citizens of Halencia.

The chancellor of the high counsel had gone to Antonio and demanded action be taken.

Antonio had flown home to advise his father the time had come. The king must abdicate and let Antonio rule or risk the monarchy being overthrown completely.

The citizens of Halencia cheered in the streets. Antonio was well loved in his home country. He lived and worked in California, but he took his duty as prince seriously. He returned home two or three times a year, maintaining a residence in Halencia and supporting many businesses and charities.

Everyone was happy. Except Tony, who had to leave everything he'd worked to achieve and go home to marry a woman he barely knew.

Zach knew the truth behind Tony's impromptu engagement four years ago. He was one of a handful of people who did. And though it was motivated by love, it wasn't for the woman he'd planned to marry.

Tony was a smart man. Zach just needed a little time to convince him that marriage was drastic and unnecessary.

Lindsay seemed like a nice person. She'd understand when this all played out. Surely she wouldn't want to bring together two people who were not meant to be a couple. Plus, she'd get paid either way. And have a nice trip to Italy for her troubles.

Once he was in Halencia and had access to Tony and Christina, he'd subtly hound them until one or the other caved to the pressure. And maybe cause a snag or two along the way so the whole thing just seemed like a bad idea.

Of course he'd have to distract the pretty wedding planner with a faux flirtation to keep her from noticing his shenanigans. No hardship there. He was attracted enough to the feisty pixie to make it fun, but she was way too picket-fence for him so there was no danger of taking it too far.

He saw it as win, win, win. Especially for those not stuck in a loveless marriage.

She lifted her glass again. "And thanks again for this program."

"I hope you like puzzles, because there's still a lot of work there."

"Not near what there was." She picked up a strawberry, dipped it in her flute and sank dainty white teeth into the fruit. The ripe juice stained her lips red and he had the keenest urge to taste the sweetness left behind. "In fact, I may actually watch the movie."

"Excellent." He all but had her eating out of his hand with that act of kindness. And he'd needed something after stumbling onto the plane half blind with a migraine and sitting on the blasted dress. He'd popped some over-the-counter meds just before boarding. Thank the flight gods the headache had finally eased off.

He needed to stick close to her if this sabotage was going to work. He'd do his best to protect her as he went forward, but if it came down to a choice between her job and the happiness of the man who meant more to him than family, he'd choose Tony every time. No matter how pretty the wedding planner.

He'd revealed more about himself than he meant

to, than he ever did really. But her attitude toward parental problems appealed to him: do what you can and move on. How refreshing to find someone who understood and accepted that not all parents were perfect. Many people didn't get along with their parents but most loved and respected them.

He tolerated his parents, but he wasn't willing to make a total break, which probably meant he harvested hope for a better relationship at some point. He couldn't imagine what might bring it about so he pretty much ignored them except when he was on the east coast or at a family function requiring his presence.

Next to him Lindsay sipped champagne and flipped through the movie choices. The dim lights caught the gold in her light brown hair. She had the thick mass rolled up and pinned in place but soft wisps had broken free to frame her face. He wondered how long the confined tresses would flow down her back. Her creamy complexion reminded him of the porcelain dolls his mother collected, complete with a touch of red in the cheeks though Lindsay's was compliments of the champagne.

She shot him a sideways glance, a question in her pretty baby blue eyes.

He realized she'd asked a question. "Sorry. I got lost in looking at you."

A flush added to the red in her cheeks and a hand pushed at the pins in her hair. "I asked if you pre-

ferred the comedy or the World War One drama."
She turned back to the screen, fidgeted with the buttons. "But maybe I should just go back to my seat."

"No. Stay. This is my celebration, after all."

She glanced at him through lush lashes. "Okay,
but you'll have to behave."

"I'll have you know my mother raised me to be
a gentleman."

"Uh-huh." She made the decision for them with
the push of a button. "That might be reassuring, except I doubt you've been under your mother's influence for quite some time."

He grinned and reached up to turn off the overhead light. "Very astute, Ms. Reeves."

Lindsay came awake to the rare sense of being
wrapped in warm, male arms. She shot straight up
in her seat, startling the man she cuddled against.
His whiskey-brown eyes opened and blinked at her,
the heat in his slumberous gaze rolling through her
like liquid fire.

Escape. Now. The words were like a beeping
alarm going off in her head.

"Can you let me out?" She pushed away from
him, gaining a few inches and hopefully reinforc-
ing the message to move. Now.

"Is the movie over?" He reined her in with an
easy strength. His broad chest lifted under her as he
inhaled a huge breath and then let it go in a yawn.

"Yes. This was fun." Too much fun. Time to get back to the real world. "But I need to get past you." He tucked a piece of her hair behind her ear instead of moving. The heat of his touch called for desperate measures. "I've got to pee."

He blinked. Then the corner of his mouth tipped up and he stood. "Me, too." He helped her up and gestured for her to go first.

"You go ahead," she urged him. "I want to grab a few things to freshen up with."

"Good idea." He opened the overhead compartment and grabbed a small bag. "Can I help you get anything?"

"Thank you, no." She waited until he wandered off to gather what she needed from her tote.

The attendants had performed her turndown service so both beds were down for the night. She automatically checked the garment bag holding the royal wedding dress. It lay nicely in place, undisturbed since the last time she checked. She bent to retrieve her tote from under the seat in front of hers and decided to take the bag with her. Strap looped over her shoulder, she hurried down the aisle.

It was after one and the people she passed appeared to be out for the count. Even the attendants were strapped in and resting. Good. Lindsay intended to take her time. She wanted Zach to be back in his seat and sound asleep when she returned.

He was too charming, too hot, too available for

her peace of mind. She hadn't needed to hear his views on marriage to know he was single. From her research she'd already gathered he had commitment issues. The only hint of an engagement had been back in his college days.

She'd found that snippet of information because she'd been researching his history with the prince. They'd both been going to Harvard's school of business but they'd met on the swim team. They both broke records for the school, Zach edging out Antonio with a few more wins. Antonio explained those extra wins came from Zach's longer reach. In the picture accompanying the article it was clear that Zach had at least three inches on all his teammates.

Tall, dark and handsome. Tick, tick, tick. The stereotype fit him to a tee, but did little to actually describe him. He was brilliant yet a terrible flirt. Could apologize when he was wrong and laugh at himself. But it was the touch of vulnerability surrounding his desire for his parents' approval that really got to her. She understood all too well the struggle between respect and love when it came to parents.

Bottom line: the man was dangerous. Way out of her league. And a distraction she couldn't afford. She may be headed for one of the most beautiful places on earth, but this was so not a vacation. She needed to stay sharp and focused to pull off the wedding of the century.

Face washed, teeth brushed, changed into yoga pants and a long-sleeved T-shirt, she glanced at her watch. Twenty minutes had passed. That should be enough time. She gathered her clothes and toiletries and tucked them neatly into her tote before making her way quietly back to her seat.

Zach lay sprawled on his bed. He was so tall he barely fit; in fact, one leg was off the bed braced against the floor. No doubt he had a restless night ahead of him. For once she'd sleep. Or pretend to. Because engaging in middle-of-the-night intimacies with Zach Sullivan could only result in trouble. Trouble she couldn't afford.

Climbing into her bed, she pulled the covers around her shoulders and determinedly closed her eyes.

She had this under control. She'd just ignore the man. If she needed something from the groom, she'd get it from the palace representative or Christina. There was no need for her to deal with Zach Sullivan at all. That suited her fine. She'd learned her lesson.

No more falling into the trap of self-delusion because a man paid a little attention to her. But more important—work and play did not go together.

"There must be some mistake." Lindsay advised the car-rental clerk. "I made my reservation over two months ago."

"*Scusa*. No mistake. My records show the reservation was canceled."

"That's impossible," Lindsay protested. Exhaustion tugged at her frayed nerves. This couldn't be happening. With everything she needed to do for the wedding, she absolutely required a vehicle to get around. "I had my assistant confirm all my reservations a week ago."

The clerk, a harried young man, glanced at the line behind her before asking with exaggerated patience, "Perhaps it is under a different name?"

"No, it is under my name." She gritted her teeth. "Please look again."

"Of course." He hit a few keys. "It says here the reservation was canceled last night."

"Last night? That doesn't make any sense at all. I was in the middle of a transatlantic flight." Enough. Arguing did her no good. She just wanted a car and to get on the road. "You know it doesn't matter. Let's just start over."

"*Scusa*, Ms. Reeves. We have no other vehicles available. Usually we would, but many have started to arrive for the royal wedding. The press especially. And they are keeping the vehicles. We have requested more autos from other sites but they won't be here for several days."

"There you are." A deep male voice sounded from behind her.

She glanced over her shoulder to find Zach towering over her. Dang, so much for losing him at the luggage carousel. Assuming her professional demeanor, she sent him a polite smile. "Have a good trip to Monte Calanetti. I'll keep you posted with updates on the arrangements. I'm going to be here for a bit." She smiled even brighter. "They've lost my car reservation."

"They didn't lose it. I canceled it."

"What?" All pretense of politeness dropped away. "Why would you do that?"

He held up a set of keys. "Because we're going to drive to Monte Calanetti together. Don't you remember? We talked about this during the movie last night."

She shook her head. She remembered him asking her what car-rental company she'd used and comparing their accommodation plans; he'd rented a villa while she had a room at a boutique hotel. Nowhere in her memory lurked a discussion about driving to Monte Calanetti together. There was no way she would have agreed to that. Not only did it go against her new decree to avoid him whenever possible, but she needed a vehicle to properly do her job.

"No," she declared, "I don't remember."

"Hmm. Must be champagne brain. No problem. I've got a Land Rover. Plenty of room for you, me and the dress." He grabbed up the garment bag, caught the handle of her larger suitcase and headed off. "Let's roll."

"Wait. No." Feeling panicked as the dress got further out of her reach, she glared at the clerk. "I want my reservation reinstated and as soon as a car is available, I want it delivered." She snatched up a card. "I'll call you with the address."

Dragging her smaller suitcase, Lindsay weaved her way through the crowd, following in Zach's wake. Luckily his height made him easy to spot. She was right on his heels when he exited the airport.

Humidity smacked her in the face as soon as she stepped outside; making her happy she'd paired her beige linen pants with a navy-and-beige asymmetrical short-sleeved tunic.

Champagne brain, her tush. What possible motive could he have for canceling her reservation if she hadn't agreed?

This just proved his potent appeal spelled danger.

Okay, no harm done. She handed him her smaller case and watched as he carefully placed the garment bag across the backseat. It should only take a couple of hours to reach Monte Calanetti. Then she could cut ties with the guy and concentrate on doing her job.

"How long to Monte Calanetti from here?" she asked as he held the door while she slid into the passenger seat.

"I've never driven it, but I can't imagine it's more than a few hours." He closed her in, rounded the front of the Land Rover and climbed into the driver's seat. A few minutes later they were in the thick of Florence traffic.

The old world elegance of the city charmed her, but the stop and go of the early evening traffic proclaimed work-force congestion was the same worldwide. She could admit, if only to herself, that she was glad not to be driving in it.

"Have you've been to Tuscany before?" she asked Zach.

"I've been several times. A couple of times with Antonio and once with my parents when I was twelve."

"So you know your way around?" She smothered a yawn.

"I do." He shot her an amused glance. "Enough to get us where we're going."

"I was just going to offer to navigate if you needed me to."

He stopped at a traffic light, taking the time to study her. "Thanks." He reached out and swept a thumb under her left eye in a soft caress. "You're tired. I guess relaxing didn't help you sleep."

She turned her head away from his touch. "I slept a little, off and on."

"Disrupted sleep can be less restful than staying awake." He sympathized. "Are you better at sleeping in a car?"

"Who can't sleep in a car? But I'm fine. I don't want to miss the sights. The city is so beautiful."

He drove with confidence and skill and a patience she lacked. He'd shaved on the plane; his sexy scruff gone when she woke this morning. The hard, square lines of his clean-cut jaw were just as compelling as the wicked shadow. The man couldn't look bad in a bag, not with a body like that.

Unlike her, he hadn't changed clothes, he still wore his black suit pants and white long-sleeved shirt, but the top two buttons were open and the sleeves were rolled up to his elbows. The suit jacket had been tossed onto the backseat.

"Florence is beautiful. The depth of history just draws me in. Halencia is the same. Since I'll be here for a month, I'm really hoping to get a chance to play tourist."

"Oh, absolutely. They have some really fantastic tours. I plan to stay after the wedding and take one. I'm torn between a chef and wine-tasting tour or a hiking tour."

"Wow, there's quite a difference there."

"I'm not going to lie to you. I'm leaning toward the pasta and wine tour. It goes to Venice. I've always wanted to go to Venice."

"Oh, yeah," he mocked, "it's all about Venice and nothing about the walking."

"Hey, I'm a walker. I love to hike. I'll share some of my brochures with you. There are some really great tours. If you like history, there's a Tuscan Renaissance tour that sounds wonderful."

"Sounds interesting. I'd like to see the brochures."

"Since technology is your thing, I'm surprised you're so into history."

"I minored in history. What can I say? I'm from New England. You can't throw a rock without hitting a historical marker. In my studies I was always amazed at how progressive our founding fathers were. Benjamin Franklin truly inspired me."

"You're kidding."

"I'm not." He sent her a chiding sidelong look. "I did my thesis on the sustainability of Franklin's inventions and observations in today's world. He was a brilliant man."

"And a great politician," she pointed out.

"I can't deny that, but he didn't let his political views define or confine him. I respect him for that. For him it wasn't about power but about proper representation."

"I feel that way about most of our founding fathers. So tell me something I probably don't know about big Ben."

"He was an avid swimmer."

"Like you and Antonio. Aha. No wonder you like him—" A huge yawn distorted the last word. "Oh." She smothered it behind a hand. "Sorry."

"No need to apologize." He squeezed her hand. "Don't feel you have to keep me company. Rest if you can. Jet lag can be a killer."

"Thanks." He'd just given her the perfect out from

having to make conversation for the next hour. She'd snap the offer up if she weren't wide-eyed over the sights. Nothing in California rivaled the history and grandeur of the buildings still standing tall on virtually every street.

Zach turned a corner and the breath caught in the back of Lindsay's throat. Brunelleschi's Dome filled the skyline in all its Gothic glory. She truly was in Italy. Oh, she wanted to play tourist. But it would have to wait. Work first.

Riding across a beautiful, sculpted old bridge, she imagined the people who once crossed on foot. Soon rural views replaced urban views and in the distance clouds darkened the sky, creating a false twilight.

Lindsay shivered. She hoped they reached Monte Calanetti before the storm hit. She didn't care for storms, certainly didn't want to get caught out in one. The turbulence reminded her of anger, the thunder of shouting. As a kid, she'd hated them.

She didn't bury her head under the covers anymore. But there were times she wanted to.

Lightning flickered in the distance. Rather than watch the storm escalate, she closed her eyes as sleep claimed her. Her last thoughts were of Zach.

Lack of motion woke Lindsay. She opened her eyes to a dark car and an eerie silence. Zach was nowhere in view. Stretching, she turned around, looking for him. No sign. She squinted out the front windshield.

Good gracious, was the hood open?

She pushed her door open and stepped out, her feet crunching on gravel as a cool wind whipped around her. Hugging herself she walked to the front of the Land Rover. Zach was bent over the engine using a flashlight to ineffectually examine the vehicle innards. "What's going on?"

"A broken belt is my best guess." He straightened and directed the light toward the ground between them. "I've already called the rental company. They're sending a service truck."

She glanced around at the unrelenting darkness. Not a single light sparkled to show a sign of civilization. "Sending a truck where? We're in the middle of nowhere."

"They'll find us. The vehicle has a GPS."

Relief rushed through her. "Oh. That's good." She'd had visions of spending the night on the side of the road in a storm-tossed tin can. "Did they say how long before they got here? *Eee!*" She started and yelped when thunder boomed overhead. The accompanying flash of lightening had her biting back a whimper to the metallic taste of blood.

"As soon as they can." He took her elbow and escorted her to the passenger's-side door. "Let's stay in the car. The storm looks like it's about to break."

His big body blocked the wind, his closeness

bringing warmth and rock-solid strength. For a moment she wanted to throw herself into his arms. Before she could give in to the urge, he helped her into her seat and slammed the door. A moment later he slid in next to her. He immediately turned the light off. She swallowed hard in a mouth suddenly dry.

"Can we keep the light on?" The question came out in a harsh rasp.

"I think we should conserve it, just in case."

"Just in case what?" It took a huge effort to keep any squeak out of her voice. "The truck doesn't come?"

"Just in case. Here—" He reached across the center console and took her hand, warming it in his. "You're shaking. Are you cold?" He dropped her hand to reach behind him. "Take my jacket."

She leaned forward and the heavy weight of his suit jacket wrapped around her shoulders. The satin lining slid coolly over her skin but quickly heated up. The scent of Zach clung to the material and she found it oddly comforting.

"Thank you. You won't be cold?"

She heard the rustle of movement and pictured him shrugging. "I'm okay right now. Hopefully the tow truck will get here before the cold seeps in. Worst case, we can move into the backseat and cuddle together under the jacket."

Okay, that option was way too tempting.

"Or you could get another one out of your luggage."

His chuckle preceded another crash of thunder. "Pixie girl, I don't know if my ego can survive you."

Maybe the dark wasn't so bad since he hadn't seen her flinch. Then his words struck her. "Pixie girl? That's the second time you called me that."

"Yes. Short and feisty. You remind me of a pixie."

"I am average," she stated with great dignity. "You're a giant."

"You barely reach my shoulder."

"Again, I refer you to the term 'giant.'" She checked her phone, welcoming the flare of light, but they were in the Italian version of Timbuktu so of course there was no service.

"Uh-huh. Feisty, pretty and short. Pixie it is."

Pretty? He'd called her that before, too. Pleasure bolstered her drooping spirits. She almost didn't care when the light faded again. Not that his admission changed her feelings toward him. He was a dangerous, charming man but she didn't have to like him just because he thought she was pretty. He was still off limits.

Hopefully he took her silence as disdain.

Right. On the positive side, the bit of vanity served to distract her for a few minutes. Long enough for headlights to appear on the horizon. No other vehicles had passed them in the twenty minutes she'd been awake so she said a little prayer that the approaching headlights belonged to their repair truck.

"Is the repair service coming from Monte Calanetti? How far away do you think we are?" She feared the thought of walking, but she didn't want to stay in the car all night, either.

"We're nowhere near Monte Calanetti," Zach announced. "By my guess we're about ten miles outside Caprese."

"Caprese?" Lindsay yelped in outrage. Caprese was the small village where the artist Michelangelo was born. "That's the other direction from Monte Calanetti from Florence. What are we doing here?"

"I told you last night. I have an errand to run for Antonio before I go to Monte Calanetti. It's just a quick stop to check on his groomsmen gifts and do a fitting."

"You so did not tell me."

"I'm pretty sure I did. You really can't hold your champagne, can you?"

"Stop saying 'champagne brain.' When did we have this conversation? Did I actually participate or was I sleeping?"

"You were talking, but I suppose you might have dozed off. You got quiet toward the end. I thought you were just involved in the movie. And then I fell asleep."

"Well, I don't remember half of what you've told me. You should have reminded me of the plans we supposedly made this morning. I need to get to Monte Calanetti and I need my own car. I know you're trying to be helpful but..."

"But I got you stuck out in the middle of nowhere. And you're already tired from the flight. I'm sorry."

Lindsay clenched her teeth in frustration watching as the headlights slowly moved closer. Sorry didn't fix the situation. She appreciated the apology—many men wouldn't have bothered—but it didn't get her closer to Monte Calanetti. She had planned to hit the road running tomorrow with a visit to the wedding venue, the Palazzo di Comparino and restored chapel, before meeting with Christina in the afternoon.

Now she'd have to reschedule, move the interview back.

"Lindsay?" Zach prompted. "Are you okay?"

"I'm trying to rearrange my schedule in my head." She glanced at her watch, which she'd already adjusted to local time. Seven-fifteen. It felt much later. "What do you think our chances are of getting to Monte Calanetti tonight?"

"Slim. I doubt we'll find a mechanic willing to work on the Land Rover tonight. We'll probably have to stay over and head out tomorrow after it's fixed."

"If they have the necessary part."

"That will be a factor, yes. Here's our help." A

small pickup honked as it drove past them then made a big U-turn and pulled up in front of them.

Zach hopped out to meet the driver.

Lindsay slid her arms into Zach's jacket and went to join them.

"Think it's the timing belt." Zach aimed his flashlight at the engine as he explained the problem to the man next to him. Their savior had gray-streaked black hair and wore blue coveralls. The name on his pocket read Luigi.

"Ciao, signora," the man greeted her.

She didn't bother to correct him, more eager to have him locate the problem than worried about his assumption that she and Zach were married.

The driver carried a much bigger flashlight. The power of it allowed the men a much better view of the internal workings of the Land Rover. The man spoke pretty good English and he and Zach discussed the timing belt and a few other engine parts, none of which Lindsay followed but she understood clearly when he said he'd have to tow them into Caprese.

Wonderful.

Luigi invited her to sit in his truck while he got the Land Rover hooked up to be towed. She nodded and retrieved her purse. Zach walked her to the truck and held the door for her. The interior smelled like grease and cleanser, but it was neat and tidy.

"From what I remember from my research of

Italy, small is a generous adjective when describing Caprese. At just over a thousand residents, 'tiny' would be more accurate. I'm not sure it has a hotel if we need to stay over."

"I'm sure there'll be someplace. I'll ask Luigi. It's starting to rain. I'm going to see if I can help him to make things go faster." He closed the door and darkness enveloped her.

The splat of rain on the windshield made her realize her ire at the situation had served to distract her from the looming storm. With its arrival, she forgot her schedule and just longed for sturdy shelter and a warm place to spend the night.

A few minutes later the men joined her. Squeezed between them on the small bench seat, she leaned toward Zach to give Luigi room to drive. The first right curve almost put her in Zach's lap.

"There's a bed-and-breakfast in town. Luigi's going to see about a room for us there." Zach spoke directly into her ear, his warm breath blowing over her skin.

She shivered. That moment couldn't come soon enough. The closer they got to town, the harder it rained. Obviously they were headed into the storm rather than away from it.

Fifteen minutes later they arrived at a small garage. Lindsay dashed through the rain to the door and then followed the men inside to an office that smelled like the truck and was just as tidy. Luigi immediately picked up the phone and dialed. He had a brief conversation in Italian before hanging up.

He beamed at Lindsay and Zach. "*Bene, bene*, my friends. The bed-and-breakfast is full with visitors. *Si*, the bad weather—they do not like to drive. But I have procured for you the last room. Is good, *si*?"

"*Si. Grazie,* Luigi." Zach expressed his appreciation then asked about the repairs.

For Lindsay only two words echoed through her head: one room.

CHAPTER FOUR

THE B AND B WAS a converted farmhouse with stone walls, long, narrow rooms and high ceilings. The furniture was sparse, solid and well worn.

Lindsay carried the heavy garment bag to the wardrobe and arranged it as best she could and then turned to face the room she'd share with Zach. Besides the oak wardrobe there was a queen bed with four posters, one nightstand, a dresser with a mirror above it and a hardback chair. Kindling rested in a fireplace with a simple wooden mantel, ready to be lit.

The bathroom was down the hall.

No sofa or chair to sleep on and below her feet was an unadorned hardwood floor. There was no recourse except to share the bed.

And the bedspread was a wedding ring quilt. Just perfect.

Her mother would say it was a sign. She'd actually have a lot more to say, as well, but Lindsay ruthlessly put a lock on those thoughts.

Lightening flashed outside the long, narrow window. Lindsay pulled the heavy drapes closed, grateful for the accommodation. She may have to share with a near stranger and the room may not be luxurious, but it was clean and authentic, and a strong, warm barrier against the elements.

Now why did that make her think of Zach?

The rain absorbed the humidity and dropped the temperature a good twenty degrees. The stone room was cool. Goose bumps chased across her skin.

She lit the kindling and once it caught added some wood. Warmth spread into the room. Unable to wait any longer, she made a quick trip down the hall. Zach was still gone when she got back. He'd dropped off her luggage and had gone back for his. She rolled the bigger case over next to the wardrobe. She didn't think she'd need anything out of it for one night.

The smaller one she set on the bed. She'd just unzipped it when a thud came at the door.

Zach surged into the room with three bags in tow.

"Oh, my goodness. You are soaked." She closed the door and rushed to the dresser. The towels were in the top drawer just as the innkeeper said.

Zach took it and scrubbed his face and head.

She tugged at his sopping jacket, glad now she'd thought to give it back to him. "Let's get this off you."

He allowed her to work it off. Under the jacket

his shirt was so damp it clung to his skin in several places. He shivered and she led him over to the fireplace.

"Oh, yeah." He draped the towel around his neck and held his hands out to the heat.

"Take the shirt off, too," she urged him. She reached out with her free hand to help with the task, but when her fingers came skin to skin with his shoulder she decided it might be best if he handled the job himself.

To avoid looking at all the tanned, toned flesh revealed by the stripping off of his shirt, Lindsay held the dripping jacket aloft. What were they going to do with it? He handed her the shirt. With them?

A knock sounded at the door. Leaving Zach by the fire, Lindsay answered the knock. A plump woman in a purple jogging suit with more gray than black in her hair gave Lindsay a bright smile.

"Si, signora." She pointed to the dripping clothes, "I take?"

"Oh. *Grazie*." Lindsay handed the wet clothes through the door.

"And these, too." From behind the door Zach thrust his pants forward.

Okay, then. She just hoped he'd kept his underwear on.

"Si, si." The woman's smile grew broader. She took the pants while craning her head to try to see

behind Lindsay. She rolled off something in Italian. Lindsay just blinked at her.

"She said the owner was sending up some food for us."

As if on cue, Lindsay's stomach gurgled. The mention of food made her realize how hungry she was. It had been hours since they'd eaten on the plane. *"Si."* She nodded. *"Grazie."*

The woman nodded and, with one last glance into the room, turned and walked down the hall.

"You have a fan." Lindsay told Zach when she closed the door. "Oh, my good dog." The man had his back to her as he leaned over the bed rummaging through his luggage. All he wore was a pair of black knit boxer briefs that clung to his butt like a lover. The soft cloth left little to the imagination and there was a lot to admire.

No wonder the maid had been so enthralled.

And Lindsay had to sleep next to that tonight.

"What about a dog?" He turned those whiskey-brown eyes on her over one broad, bare shoulder.

Her knees went weak, nearly giving out on her. She sank into the hard chair by the fire.

"Dog? Huh? Nothing." Her mother had taught her to turn the word around so she didn't take the Lord's name in vain. After all these years, the habit stuck.

He tugged on a gray T-shirt.

Thank the merciful angels in heaven.

"I'm going to take a quick shower. Don't eat all the food."

"No promises."

He grinned. "Then I'll just have to hurry."

He disappeared out the door with his shaving kit under one arm and the towel tossed over his shoulder.

Finally Lindsay felt as though she could breathe again.

He took up so much space. A room that seemed spacious one moment shrank by three sizes when he crossed the threshold. Even with him gone the room smelled of him.

She patted her pocket. Where was her phone? She needed it now, needed to call the rental agency that very moment and demand a car be delivered to her. They should never have allowed a party outside the reservation to cancel. They owed her.

The hunt proved futile. Her phone wasn't in her purse, her tote or either suitcase. She thought back to the last time she'd used it. In the Land Rover, where it had been pitch-black. It must still be in the vehicle.

That was at the garage.

There'd be no getting her phone tonight. Dang it.

Stymied from making the call she wanted to, she took advantage of Zach's absence to gather her own toiletries and yoga pants and long-sleeved tee she'd worn on the plane. And a pair of socks. Yep, she'd wear gloves to bed if she had any with her. And if she had any luck at all, he'd wear a three-piece suit.

There'd be no skin-to-skin contact if she could help it.

Loosen up, Lindsay. Her mom's voice broke through her blockade. *You're young and single and about to share a bed with one prime specimen. You should be thinking of ways to rock the bed not bulletproof yourself against an accidental touch.*

How sad was it that her mother was more sexually aggressive than she was?

Her mom was forever pushing Lindsay to date more, to take chances on meeting people. She'd been thrilled when Lindsay had started seeing Kevin again. She'd welcomed him; more, she'd invited him to family events and made a point of showing her pride in Lindsay and her success.

Right, and look how that turned out.

To be fair, Mom had been almost as devastated as Lindsay when Kevin showed his true colors. She may be self-absorbed but Lindsay never doubted her mom's love. She wanted Lindsay to be happy and in her mind that equated to love and marriage. Because for her it was—at least during the first flush of love.

Lindsay wanted to believe in love and happily ever after, but it was getting harder to do as she planned her mother's sixth wedding. And, okay, yeah, Mom was right; Lindsay really didn't make an effort to meet men. But that wasn't the problem.

She actually met lots of interesting men. While she was working, when it was totally inappropriate to pursue the connection.

The problem was she was too closed off when she did meet a nice guy. After stepfather number two, she'd started putting up shields to keep from being hurt when they left. She and Kevin had been friends before they were a couple and when they'd split up, her shields just grew higher.

She hadn't given up on love. She just didn't know if she was brave enough to reach for it.

You're in Italy for a month with a millionaire hunk at your beck and call. It's the perfect recipe for a spicy summer fling. Every relationship doesn't have to end with a commitment.

Mom didn't always practice what she preached.

The food hadn't arrived when Zach returned smelling of freshly washed male. He wore the same T-shirt but now his knit boxers were gray. She could only thank the good Lord—full-on prayer, here—that the T-shirt hung to his thighs, hiding temptation from view.

"Bathroom is free," he advised her.

Her stomach gurgled, but he looked so relaxed after his shower and the storm had her so on edge she decided to get comfortable. Grabbing up the cache she'd collected, she headed for the door.

"Don't eat all the food," she told him.

"Hey, you get the same promise I did."

She stared at him a moment trying to determine if he was joking as she'd been. His features were impassive and he cocked a dark brow at her. Hmm. She better hurry just in case.

The bathroom was still steamy from his visit. As she pulled the shower curtain closed on the tiny tub she envisioned his hard body occupying this same space. His hard, wet, naked body. Covered in soap bubbles.

Oh. My. Dog.

She forced her mind to the nearly completed seating chart to remove him from her head. But that, too, reminded her of him so she switched to the flowers. Christina had yet to decide between roses and calla lilies or a mix of the two. Both were beautiful and traditional for weddings.

It may well depend on the availability. Christina wanted to use local vendors and merchants. She'd said it was for the people so should be of the people. Lindsay still puzzled over the comment. *It* was obviously the wedding, but what did she mean "it was for the people"?

Was the royal wedding not a love match?

Lindsay could ask Zach. He'd know.

No. She didn't want to know. It was none of her business and may change how she approached the wedding. Every bride deserved a fantasy wedding, one that celebrated the bond between her and the groom and the promise of a better future together.

It was Lindsay's job to bring the fantasy to life. The reality of the relationship was not in her hands.

Her musings took her through the shower, a quick attempt at drying her hair, brushing her teeth and dressing. Fifteen minutes after she left the room, she returned to find Zach seated on the bed, his back against the headboard, a tray of food sitting beside him.

The savory aroma almost brought her to her knees.

"Oh, that smells good." She dropped her things into her open case, flipped the top closed and set it on the floor before climbing onto the bed to bend over the tray and the two big bowls it held. She inhaled deeply, moaned softly. "Soup?"

"Stew."

"Even better. And bread." She looked at him. "You waited."

He lifted one shoulder and let it drop. "Not for long. It just got here. Besides, we're partners."

Her eyebrows shot up then lowered as she scowled at him. "We are so not partners." She handed him a bowl and a spoon. Tossed a napkin in his lap. Then settled cross-legged on her pillow and picked up her own bowl. "In fact, I think I should arrange for my own car tomorrow. I need to get to Monte Calanetti and you have to wait for the Land Rover to be repaired, which could take a couple of days."

"Getting a car here could take longer yet. You

heard the rental clerk. All the vehicles are being taken up by the media presence here for the wedding."

"Oh, this is good." No point in arguing with him. She was an adult and a professional. She didn't require his permission to do anything.

"Mmm." He hummed his approval. "Are you okay with sharing?"

"The room?" She shrugged. "We don't really have a choice, do we?"

"The bed," he clarified and licked his spoon. She watched, fascinated. "I can sleep on the floor if you're uncomfortable sharing the bed."

"It's hardwood." She pulled her gaze away from him. "And there isn't any extra bedding."

"I can sleep near the fireplace. It won't be comfortable, but I'll survive. We're still getting to know each other, so I'll understand."

Crack!

Thunder boomed, making Lindsay jump and spill the bite of stew aimed for her mouth.

"Dang it." She grabbed her napkin and scrubbed at the stain on her breast. "Are you uncomfortable?"

"No." He took her bowl so she could use both hands. "But I'm a man."

Oh, yeah, she'd noticed.

"If something happened between us, I'd be a happy man in the morning. You, on the other hand, would be satisfied but regretful."

She glared at him. "Nothing is going to happen."

He held up his hands, the sign of surrender blemished by the bowls he held. "Of course not."

"So there's no reason not to share."

"None at all."

"It's settled then."

"Yep." He handed her bowl back. "Now you want to tell me what your deal is with storms?"

Zach watched the color leech from Lindsay's cheeks, confirmation that his suspicions were right that her reaction to the thunderstorm exceeded the norm.

She was nervous and jumpy, which was totally unlike her.

Sure she'd gone ballistic when he'd sat on the wedding dress, but considering the cost of the gown she could be forgiven for hyperventilating.

Generally he found her to be calm and collected, giving as good as she got but not overreacting or jumping to conclusions. Efficient but friendly. The storm had her shaken and he wanted to know why.

"Nothing." She carefully placed her bowl on the tray. "I'm fine."

"You're jumpy as hell. And it started before we got to the room so it isn't the sleeping arrangements. It has to be the storm."

"Maybe it's you." She tossed the words at him as she slid from the bed. "Did you consider that?"

"Nope." His gaze followed her actions as she put

the suitcase back on the bed and began to organize the things she'd dumped in. "We're practically lovers."

Ice burned cold in the blue glare she sent him. "You are insane."

"Oh, come on." He taunted her. "You know it's going to happen. Not tonight, but definitely before the month is up."

"In your dreams. But I live in reality."

"Tell me about the storms."

"There's nothing to tell." The jerkiness of her movements told a different story.

"Okay. Have it your way." He relaxed back against the wall and laced his arms behind his head. "I like storms myself."

"You like storms?" The astonishment in her voice belied her indifference. "As I said, insane. I'm going to take the tray downstairs."

Zach grabbed the bread and wine from the tray and let her escape. Pressing her would only antagonize her.

He'd had nothing to do with the engine failure, but he approved of the results. If he were a man who believed in signs, he'd take it as karma's righteous nod.

He'd been playing with her when he'd alluded to them being lovers. Or so he thought. As soon as the words had left his mouth, he'd known the truth in them. He generally preferred leggy blondes. But something about the pixie appealed to him.

Her feistiness certainly. At the very least it was refreshing. With his position, family connections and money, people rarely questioned his authority and never dismissed him. She'd done both. And still was.

He had no doubt she'd try to make a break for it tomorrow.

He sipped at the last of his wine, enjoyed the warmth as it rolled down his throat. The fire had burned down to embers and he stirred himself to get up and feed it. The thick stone walls and bare wood floors kept the room cool so the fire gave nice warmth to the room. Plus, he imagined Lindsay would find it a comforting offset to the storm.

She was more pretty than beautiful, her delicate features overshadowed by that lush mouth. His gut tightened as heat ignited his blood just as flame flared over the fresh fuel.

Oh, yeah, he wanted a bite of that plump lower lip.

He'd have to wait. He'd put her off limits when he concocted the sabotage plan. He couldn't use her and seduce her, too. That would be too much. But she didn't need to know of his restraint. Just the thought of him making a move on her would keep her on edge, making it easier for him to cause a little chaos.

A glance at his watch showed the time at just after nine. Early for him to go to bed most nights but tonight, fatigue from travel, the time change and the concentration needed to drive an unfamiliar vehicle on unfamiliar roads weighed on him.

The room held no TV so it was sleep or talk.

He wouldn't mind getting to know his companion better but somehow he knew she'd choose the escape that came with sleep. Whether she actually slept or not. His feisty little pixie had a bit of the ostrich in her.

The door opened and she slipped inside.

"You're still up?" She avoided his gaze as she crossed to the bed and zipped the case that still sat on her side.

"Just feeding the fire."

She lifted the case and he stepped forward to take it from her.

"I can do it," she protested, independent as always.

"So can I." He notched his chin toward the bed. "You're falling asleep on your feet. Go to bed."

"What about you?" Caution filled her voice and expression.

"I'm going to tend the fire for a bit. I'll come to bed soon."

Relief filled her blue eyes and he knew she thought she'd gotten a reprieve; that she hoped to be asleep before he joined her in the far too small bed.

Truthfully, he hoped she fell asleep, too. No point in both of them lying awake thinking about the other.

Lindsay pretended to be asleep when Zach came to bed. His presence kept her senses on edge. Between him and the storm that still raged outside her nerves were balanced on a fine-edged sword.

She tried to relax, to keep her breathing even so as not to disturb Zach. The last thing she wanted was another discussion on why storms bothered her. It was a weakness she preferred to ignore. She usually plugged in her earphones and let her playlist tune out the noise.

Tonight there was nothing in the still house to disguise the violence of the weather outside the window. Everything in her longed to press back into the strong male body occupying the other half of the bed. Instead she clung to the edge of the mattress determined to stay on her side.

Thunder boomed and lightening strobed at the edges of the closed drapes. Lindsay flinched then held herself very still.

"Oh, for the love of dog, come here." Long, muscular arms wrapped around her and tugged her against the hard planes of a male chest.

Shocked by both action and words, Lindsay chose to focus on the latter. She glanced over her shoulder into dark eyes. "What did you say?"

"Woof, woof." And his lips settled softly on her cheek, a simple human-to-human contact that left her wanting more.

She sighed and made a belated attempt to wiggle away. Her body and nerves might welcome his touch but her head shouted, *Danger!* "I know it's silly. It's something my mom taught me when I was little. It kind of stuck."

"I think it's cute."

She went still. "I'm not cute. I'm not a pixie. And we're not going to be lovers. You need to let me go." One of them needed to be smart about this.

His arms tightened, pulled her back the few inches she'd gained. "Tell me about the storms."

"There's nothing to tell!"

His silence was a patient demand.

"What's to like about them? They're angry and destructive."

"A storm is cleansing. It can be loud, yes, but it takes the old and washes it clean."

She thought about that. "Destruction is not cleansing."

"It can be. If something is rotten or breaking, it's better to come down in a storm than under a person's weight. You might have to finish the cleanup but life is fresher once you're done."

"I doubt people who have lost their homes to a hurricane or tornado would agree with you."

"Hurricanes and tornadoes are different. This is

a simple summer thunderstorm. Nothing to get so worked up over."

"I know." She lay with her cheek pressed against her hand. She should move away, put space and distance between them. But she didn't. Couldn't. Having strong arms surrounding her gave her a sense of belonging she hadn't experienced in way too long. It didn't even matter that it was all in her head. Her body had control right now. With a soft sigh she surrendered to his will and her body's demand.

"It's not even my phobia. It's my mother's that she passed on to me." She blamed the kiss for loosening her resolve. Hard to keep her wits about her with the heat of his kiss on her cheek.

"How'd she do that?"

"She hates storms. They don't scare her, though, they make her cry."

"Why?"

"She was only seventeen when she got pregnant with me. My dad tried to step up and they got married, even though he was barely eightteen. My mom is very high maintenance. Her dad always gave her everything she wanted. Took care of things for her. She expected my dad to do the same. She was too demanding and he finally left. It was during a storm that he took off and never came back. She was left pregnant and alone."

"So she cries when it rains."

"Yes." Lindsay had pieced the story together

through the years. She loved her mother; she was fun and free-spirited. But Lindsay also recognized her faults; it had been a matter of self-preservation.

"Her dislike of storms comes from sadness."

She nodded, her hair brushing over his chin. She'd never talked to anyone about this.

"But your jumpiness suggests a fear-based reaction."

A shiver racked her body and she curled in on herself. Everything in her tightened, shutting down on a dark memory. She wanted to tell him it was none of his business, but then he might let her go and she wasn't ready to give up the cocoon of his embrace.

His arms tightened around her and his lips slid over her cheek, giving her the courage to answer.

"It's a lingering unease leftover from childhood. It's distressing to hear your mother cry and know there's nothing you can do to help."

"It seems the mother should be comforting the child, not the other way around."

"She's more sensitive than I am."

A tender touch tucked her hair behind her ear, softly trailed down the side of her neck. "Just because you're tough doesn't mean you don't need reassurance now and again."

She relaxed under the gentle attention. Though she rejected the truth in his words.

"This storm caught me when I was tired. I'm

sorry I disturbed you. I usually put my earbuds in but I left my phone in the Land Rover."

"Ah, a sensible solution. I should have known." He shifted behind her, leaving her feeling chilled and alone. And then his weight settled against her again and earbuds entered her ears. "You're stuck with my playlist, but maybe it'll help you sleep."

She smiled and wrapped her hand around his. "Thank you."

His fingers squeezed hers.

She felt the tension drain away. Now she had the music, she'd be okay. She no longer needed the comfort of his arms.

Her eyes closed. In a minute she'd pull away. There was danger in staying too close to him. Already her body recognized his, which made it all too easy for him to hold sway over her. She needed to stay strong, to stay distant...

The last thing she knew was the feel of his lips on her cheek.

CHAPTER FIVE

LINDSAY WOKE JUST before eight with the earbuds still in her ears. The tunes had stopped. She felt around for the phone but came up with the end of the earbuds instead. Her hand hadn't encountered a hard male body, but the stillness of the room had already told her Zach was out and about.

She threw back the covers and her feet hit the floor, her toes curling in her socks against the chill of the hardwood. Padding to the window, she pushed back the drapes to a world awash in sunshine. The ground was still wet but the greenery and rock fences had a just-scrubbed brightness to them.

Or was that Zach's influence on her?

A peek down the hall showed the bathroom was free so she quickly grabbed her things and made a mad dash to claim it. Aware others may be in need of the facilities she kept it short and soon returned to the room to dress and put on her makeup.

Before going downstairs, she packed her things so she'd be ready to leave when a car arrived. In spite of Zach's comfort and kindness last night, or maybe because of it, she fully intended to make her break from him today.

The heavenly scent of coffee greeted her in the dining room. Some fellow occupants of the B and B were seated at the long wooden table, including Zach. Cheerful greetings came her way as she moved through the room.

"Breakfast is buffet style this morning as there're so many of us." A gray-haired gentleman pointed with his fork toward the buffet she'd passed.

"Henry, don't use your utensils to point." An equally gray-haired woman pushed his hand down. "They'll think we have no manners." She smiled at Lindsay with a mouth full of crooked teeth. "That handsome husband of yours made you a cup of coffee he was about to take upstairs. I'm glad you could join us. I'm happy to meet up with some fellow Americans. We're Wes and Viv Graham from Iowa and the folks there on the end are Frank and Diane Murphy from Oregon."

"Nice to meet you all." She sent Zach a questioning look at the husband comment and received a shrug in reply. Right. She'd get him for that. Hopefully they wouldn't be there long enough for it to be an issue. She backtracked to the buffet.

Croissants, sausage, bacon, quartered oranges and some cappuccino. No eggs. She took a couple of pieces of bacon, one sausage and a few orange wedges.

"I was just about to come wake you." Zach appeared beside her and took her plate. "I've arranged for alternate transportation and it'll be here in about half an hour. How'd you sleep?"

Huh. If he was leaving in half an hour maybe she'd stick with him, after all. It would take her longer than that to get her phone. "I slept well, thank you." Truly thanks to him.

"You're going to want one of these." He placed a croissant on her plate. "It's called a *cornetto*. There's a wonderful jam inside."

He took off for his seat, leaving her to follow. Their audience watched with avid curiosity. At their end of the table, Lindsay smoothed her hand across his shoulders. "Thank you, sweetie." She kissed him softly, lingering over his taste for a beat longer than she intended to, then slid into the chair around the corner to his right.

She pressed her lips together. Okay, that bit of payback totally backfired. But playing it through to the end, she glanced shyly down the table. "I'm sorry. We don't mean to be rude. Newlyweds." She rolled her eyes as if that explained everything.

A pleased smile bloomed on Diane's face. "Oh, my dear, don't mind us old folks. Congratulations. You two enjoy yourselves." She turned to her husband. "Frank do you remember on our honeymoon when we—"

"Well done." Zach pushed her coffee toward her. "But that's the first and last time you ever call me sweetie."

She flashed him a provocative look. "We'll see."

Let him stew on that. He was the one to say they'd be lovers, after all.

"Be nice to me or I'll take your *cornetto*."

"I don't think so." She picked up the horn-shaped pastry and bit in. Chewed. Savored. "Oh, my dog."

"I told you so." Satisfaction stamped his features as he leaned back in his straight-backed chair.

"This is wonderful." She pointed at the jam-filled roll. "We have to have these at the wedding."

"We're a long way from Monte Calanetti."

"Oh, I'm aware." Censure met unrepentance. "Tell me again why we're in Caprese and not Monte Calanetti?"

"An errand for the prince."

She waited for more. It didn't come.

"I took care of it this morning. I'm ready to go when the new transportation gets here."

That was a relief. She finished the last of her *cornetto* with a regretful sigh and a swipe of her tongue over her thumb. "Maybe not these exact rolls but definitely *cornettos*."

"I'm all for it, but I suggest you discuss that with Christina."

She nodded, eyeing him speculatively through another bite. "How well do you know Christina?"

"Not well." He glanced down, snagged one of her orange wedges. "I met her once. Theirs has been a long-distance relationship."

"She seems really nice. And she showed a lot of enthusiasm when we first started planning, but she's cooled off lately."

"Really?" That brought his head up. "Do you think she's having second thoughts?"

Lindsay gave a half shrug. "Very few brides make it to the altar without suffering a few nerves along the way. It's probably nothing. Or nothing to do with the wedding, anyway."

"Tony's been off, too. He got me to come all this way a month in advance of the wedding, but now it feels like he's avoiding me."

"I'm sure they both have a lot on their plates right now." So much for the reassurances she'd been hoping for. The fact Zach had noticed something off, too, gave her some concerns. "I'll know more after my appointment with Christina, which was supposed to be this afternoon. I'll have to reschedule. Oh, that reminds me. I need to get my phone out of the Land Rover."

"Sorry, I forgot." Zach reached around and pulled something from his back pocket. He set her phone on the table. "I had Luigi bring it by this morning."

"Thanks." She picked it up, felt the warmth of the

glass and metal against her flesh and tried to disengage from the fact it had absorbed the heat from his hot bum.

A loud whopping sound overhead steadily got louder. Everyone looked up. Then, in an unchoreographed move, they all stood and rushed to the back terrace. Lindsay, with Zach on her heels, brought up the rear.

As she stepped out onto the cobblestone patio, a helicopter carefully maneuvered in the air, preparing to land in the large farmyard.

Zach watched Lindsay's face as the big bird neared the ground, knew by the pop of her eyes exactly when she spied the royal insignia on the door. She turned to stare at him as the inn occupants wandered forward to examine the helicopter and talk to the pilot.

Zach surveyed the royal conveyance with a smirk. "Our new transportation."

"You have got to be kidding me."

He liked the look of awe in her eyes. Much better than the fear she'd tried so hard to hide the night before. There was something more to her dislike of storms than a leftover agitation from her mother's distress. Something she wasn't willing to share, or maybe something she didn't fully remember.

He wished he could have done more than just lend her his earbuds.

"It's good to have friends in high places. When I

told Tony you were concerned about missing your appointment with Christina, he insisted on putting the helicopter at my disposal in assisting you for the duration."

Actually, Zach had suggested it; still Tony jumped at the chance to accommodate Christina. Forget bending over backward, Tony was doing flips to give Christina the wedding of her dreams. Because he knew their lives were going to suck.

For Zach's part, he figured the sooner he got to Christina, the sooner he could talk sense into her. They'd only met once, but Tony lauded her with being a sensible, caring person. Surely she saw the error in what they were about to do.

He could only hope she'd listen to reason and end things now. Then he and the wedding planner could spend the next month exploring the wonders of Tuscany.

Shock had her staring wide-eyed at the big machine. "I have a helicopter for the next month?"

"I have a helicopter until after the wedding. The pilot takes his orders from me."

"Ah. But you're here to help me." She rubbed her hands together. "So, I have my very own helicopter for the next month. Oh, this is going to make things so much easier."

"I'm glad you're happy." And glad he'd be able to keep tabs on her. Things were falling nicely into place. "I told him I had designs on his wedding planner and I needed something to impress her."

All wonder dropped away in a heartbeat.

His little pixie turned fierce, getting right up in his space.

"Listen to me, Mr. Sullivan." Her blue-diamond eyes pinned him to the spot. "You may not think much of what I do, but it's very important to me, to your friends and, in the case of this wedding, to this country. I was starting to like you, but mess with my business and you won't like me."

Dog, she was beautiful. She may be tiny but she worked that chin and those eyes. He'd never wanted to kiss a woman more in his life. Defensive, yes, but not just for herself. She honestly cared about Tony and Christina. And the blasted country.

He did like her. More than he should. He'd have to be careful not to damage her in his rescue mission.

"Tony is why I'm here. Ms. Reeves. I promise you, I'm going to do everything in my power to make sure this turns out right for him."

"Okay, then." Her posture relaxed slightly. "As long as we understand each other."

"Understand this." He wrapped his hands around her elbows, lifted her to her toes and slanted his mouth over hers.

She stiffened against him for the briefest moment, in the next all her luscious softness melted into him. She opened her mouth to his and the world dropped away. The sparkling-clean farmyard, chattering Midwest tourists and his majesty's royal helicopter disappeared from his radar.

He'd meant the kiss to be a distraction, to focus her on his mythical seduction and away from his actual plan to change Tony's mind about marrying Christina. And vice versa.

But all he knew in that moment, all he wanted to know, was the heated touch of the pixie coming apart in his arms. He wrapped her close, angling the kiss to a new depth. She tasted of berry jam and spicy woman. Her essence called to him, addled his senses until he craved nothing more than to sweep her into his arms and carry her up to their room.

Her arms were linked around his neck and he'd dragged her up his body so they were pressed together mouth to mouth, chest to chest, loins to loins. It wasn't enough. It was too much.

Someone patted him on the arm. "You young ones need to take that upstairs."

The world came crashing back. Zach slowly broke off the kiss. He lifted his head, opened his eyes. Passion-drenched pools of blue looked back at him. Her gaze moved to his mouth. A heavy sigh shifted her breasts against his chest. She looked back at him and blinked.

"You should put me down now."

Yes, he should. The kiss had gotten way out of

control and he needed to rein it in. "I don't want to. Christina will understand if we're an hour late."

What was he saying? *Get a grip, Sullivan.*

"I won't." She pushed against him. "This was a mistake. And it won't happen again."

"Why not?" he demanded because that's what he'd want to know if he were seriously pursuing her, which he wasn't. She was too sweet, too genuine for him. He needed someone who knew the rules of non-commitment.

Still, when he set her on her feet, he took satisfaction in the fact he had to steady her for a moment.

"Because I'm a professional. Because you are the best man."

"And you have a policy. You're the boss, you can change policy."

"Not a good idea." She straightened her shirt, smoothing the fabric over her hips. "I have the policy for a reason. I'm the wedding planner. I'm not here to have fun. I'm here to work. You—" she swept him with a glance "—would be a distraction when I need all my wits about me."

"Signor..." The pilot approached. "If you desire to stick to your flight plan, we should leave within the next fifteen minutes."

"Thank you."

"May I assist with the luggage?"

Glad to have this scene wrapping to a close, Zach met her gaze. "Are you ready?"

"I am." She stepped back, composed herself. "I just need to grab my luggage and the wedding dress." She headed into the house. "Do you think they'd mind if I took a few *cornettos* to go?"

Grinning, he followed her inside. He best be careful or this woman was going to turn him inside out.

Lindsay loved traveling by helicopter. She'd been a little nervous to start out with, afraid the heights might get to her. Nope. Whizzing through the air above the scenic vista gave her a thrill.

The helicopter flew over a meadow that looked like gold velvet. She pointed. "It's beautiful. What crop is that?"

"No crop, *signorina*." The pilot's voice came over her headphones. "Sunflowers."

"Sunflowers," she breathed. She'd never seen a whole field of the big, cheerful flowers.

Zach tapped the pilot on the shoulder and he took them down and did a wide loop so she actually saw the flowers. She'd told Zach she wasn't there to have fun, but, oh, she was.

That didn't mean she could throw caution to the wind and jump into a summer fling. Her blood still thrummed from his embrace. It would have been so easy to let him seduce her. Except she couldn't. She needed to grow a spine, put him in his place. The problem was she melted as soon as he touched her.

If she was honest, the physical attraction wasn't

what worried her. She liked him. Way too much for her peace of mind. That made the physical all the more tempting. She wanted love in her life but this was the wrong time, wrong place, wrong man.

Restraint came at a cost, but she wouldn't jeopardize everything she'd built on an overload of hormones. She just needed to resist him for a few weeks and then she'd be back in Hollywood and he'd be back in Silicon Valley.

Zach pointed out the palace as they flew over Voti, Halencia's capital city and Christina's home. The big, yellow palace presented a majestic silhouette with its square shape and the round battlement towers at the corners. The notched alternate crenels screamed castle. The building had a strong, regal presence set on a shallow cliff side overlooking the sea on one side and the sprawling city of Voti on the other.

One of the towers had been converted into a heliport.

"Are we landing at the palace?" She spoke into the microphone attached to the headphones.

"Yes." Zach nodded.

"So I'll get a chance to meet Prince Antonio?"

Now he shook his head. "Sorry, he's in meetings all day. We'll be going straight down and out to a car waiting for us. We'll be just in time for your one-thirty appointment with Christina."

The helicopter made a wide turn then started its

descent. Lindsay experienced her first anxious moments, seeing the land rush up to meet her. Without thinking, she reached out and grabbed Zach's hand.

His warm grip wrapped around her fingers and gave a squeeze. She instantly relaxed, feeling grounded. Putting her stringent, no-fraternizing policy aside for a moment, she smiled at him. He'd been gentle and kind last night and was supportive now. No doubt he'd hate the description, but he was a genuinely good guy.

Even though she was essentially a stranger to him, Zach had gone over and beyond the call of duty.

She longed to see some of the interior of the palace, but a palace attendant met them and a very modern elevator took them straight down to the ground level. The attendant led them through a ten-foot portico, which he explained was the width of the castle walls.

Wow, Lindsay mouthed. Seriously, she felt like a little girl at Disneyland. She was so busy trying to see everything at once she nearly tripped over her own feet.

Zach grasped her elbow. Steadied her. "Careful, Tinkerbell."

Caught gawking. But she couldn't care. This was amazing. "We're in a castle. Couldn't I be Cinderella?"

He released her to tug on her straight ponytail. "No changing up now. Tinkerbell is a pixie, right?"

"She's a fairy. And you need to stop. I'm not that short."

"You're a little bitty thing. With lots of spunk. Nothing bad about that."

She rolled her eyes. "If you say so." They exited onto a round driveway where a car and driver waited. She grabbed Zach's arm to stop him. "Listen, you don't need to come to my appointment with Christina. I can promise you'll be monumentally bored. If you stay here, you may get a few minutes to visit with Antonio."

"I want to come. It'll be good to see Christina again and to let her know Antonio isn't shirking his groom duties." He waved the driver off and held the door open for her himself. "Besides, I'm not hanging around hours just to get a few minutes of Tony's time. We'll connect soon enough."

She should go through her notes on the ride through Voti to be prepared for the appointment. Should, but wouldn't. The city was so charming, not a high-rise to be seen, and the buildings were bunched closely together, creating narrow lanes. The warmth of the earth tones and red-tiled roofs was like an architectural hug. She loved the bursts of color in hanging planters. And the odd little plazas they'd drive through that all had lovely little fountains.

Christina worked not far from the palace. All too soon the car pulled to a stop in front of a three-story building. Lovely, black, wrought-iron gates opened into a cobblestoned courtyard.

"Zach, Ms. Reeves, welcome." The driver must have called ahead because Christina stepped forward to greet them.

She was tall—Lindsay's notes read five nine and her subtle heels added a few inches to that—and stunning with creamy, olive skin and thick reddish-brown hair sleeked back in a French twist. She wore a fitted suit in cobalt blue.

Standing between her and Zach, Lindsay did feel short.

"Christina." Zach wrapped her hand in both of his. "You haven't changed a bit in four years."

"You flatter me," she said in perfect English, her accent charming. She led them through the courtyard and up a curving wrought-iron staircase to an office on the second floor. "We both know that's not true. Thank goodness. I was barely out of school and quite shy."

"And soon you'll be the Queen of Halencia."

Christina's eyelashes flickered and she looked down as she waved them into seats. "I prefer to focus on one thing at a time. First there is the wedding."

"Of course."

"Thank you, Ms. Reeves, for coming so early to

assist in the preparations. I originally intended to continue with the foundation on a part-time basis in their offices here in Halencia, but the prince's advisors have convinced me I'll be quite busy. It would be unfair to the foundation to hold a position and not be here to help. It is such a worthy endeavor. I would not want to hamper it in any way."

"It's important work. I'm sure, as the queen, your interest will be quite beneficial, so you'll still be of help."

"That's kind of you to say." Christina inclined her head.

A regal gesture if Lindsay had ever seen one. Maybe she'd been practicing.

Lindsay waved toward the open window. "You have a lovely view of the palace from here. It must be amazing to sit here and see your future beckoning for you."

Christina's smile slipped a little. "Yes. Quite amazing."

"It's a lot to think about, isn't it?" Zach spoke softly. "All that you're giving up. All that you're taking on?"

Appalled at the questions that were sure to rattle the most confident of brides let alone one showing a slight nervousness, Lindsay sent him a quelling glance.

"I am at your disposal to assist in any way I can," she advised her bride.

"You have been wonderful. My mind is just everywhere these days. I hope you do not mind taking on the bulk of the arrangements?"

"Of course. If we can just make some final decisions, I can take care of everything. Your attendants are all set, the dresses have been received and a first fitting completed. I just need to know your final thoughts on the flowers, the total head count and whether you want to do indoors or outdoors for the reception. I have some sketches for you to look at." She passed a slim portfolio across the desk. "The palace wants to use the royal photographer, but I know some truly gifted wedding photographers if you decide you want a specialist."

"I am sure the royal photographer will be fine. These are marvelous drawings, Ms. Reeves. Any of these settings will be wonderful."

"Lindsay." She gently corrected the soon-to-be princess, who seemed near tears as she looked at the reception scenes. Lindsay could tell she wasn't going to get much more from the woman. "Every wedding should be special. What can I do to make your day special?"

"You have done so much already. I like the outdoors. I remember playing in the palazzo courtyard, pretending it was a palace. It seems appropriate."

"Outdoors is a lovely choice. Regarding flowers, we passed a meadow of sunflowers on our way here today. Gold is one of the royal colors you listed. I wondered—"

"Sunflowers! Yes, I would love that. And roses, I think. You seem to know what I want better than I do."

"I've done this for a long time. I'll get the final head count from the palace contact. We've covered almost everything. But we never addressed if they do the traditional 'something old, something new, something borrowed, something blue' here in Halencia or if you even want to play along?"

"What is this tradition?" A frown furrowed her delicate brow.

"It's just a fun tradition that originated in England. It represents continuity, promise of the future, borrowed happiness and love, purity and fidelity."

"It sounds quite lovely. But I do not have any of these things."

"The fun is in getting them. In America the items are often offered by friends and family. If you share you're doing this, you'll get everything you need and it will all have special meaning for you."

"I know of something old." She tapped a finger against her desk. "Yes, I would like to have it for the wedding. It is a brooch that has been in my father's family for many years. It is said that those who wore the brooch at their wedding enjoyed many happy years together. Yes. I must have the brooch."

"Sounds perfect." Pleased to get a positive reaction and some enthusiasm from the bride, Lindsay made a note in her tablet.

"But I do not know where the brooch is." Sadness drained the brief spark of light. "The women of my generation have not chosen to go with the old tradition. Do you think you can help me find it?" Christine's eyes pleaded with Lindsay. "My grandmother or Aunt Pia might know who had it last."

Goodness, Lindsay never liked to say no to a bride, but she couldn't see how her schedule would accommodate hours on the phone tracking down a lost family jewel.

"Sure, we'll be happy to locate it for you."

Zach stole her opportunity to respond. But, sure, it was a good way to keep him occupied and out of her hair.

"We're talking a few phone calls, right?"

Christina shook her head. "The older generation of women in my family are very traditional. They will not talk of such things to a stranger over the phone. And they will not talk to you alone, Zach." She reached for a pen and paper. "I will write a letter you can take with you. *Grazie*, both of you."

Oh, Zach, what had he got them into? The hope in Christina's eyes prevented Lindsay from protesting time constraints.

"I wish I could give you more time but with learning the workings of the palace, I am a bit overwhelmed." Christina handed Lindsay the letter she'd written. "With the two of you helping, I feel so much better."

"I'm glad." Lindsay tucked the letter into her tote.

"Lindsay, do you mind if I have a moment alone with Christina?" Zach made the quiet demand and tension instantly radiated from his companion.

"Of course." Lindsay stood and offered her hand to Christina. "I'll keep you apprised of the arrangements."

"Thank you." Christina used both hands to convey her urgency. "And the progress in locating the brooch."

"Absolutely." Lindsay smiled and turned away. With her back to Christina, Lindsay narrowed her eyes at him and mouthed the words, "Do not upset the bride."

He maintained an impassive demeanor. "I'll be along in a moment."

Though Christina watched him expectantly, he waited for the distinct click of the door closing before he addressed her.

"I hope you'll forgive my concern, but I noticed you seem unsettled."

"I have much on my mind."

"I understand. But I also know the circumstances of your…relationship with Antonio." The situation warranted discretion on so many levels. "And I wonder if you're having second thoughts?"

Her chin lifted in a defensive gesture. "No."

"Perhaps you should."

Surprise showed before she composed her features into a calm facade. "I can assure you I have considered the matter thoroughly. Did Antonio send you here to test me?"

"No. Tony has asked me to be his advocate in all things wedding related. I take my responsibilities seriously and when I look at this situation, I have to wonder what the two of you are thinking. Marriage is a binding, hopefully lifelong, commitment. The two of you barely know each other. No one would blame you if you changed your mind. Least of all Tony. He knows how much you've already sacrificed for your country."

Her shoulders went back. "Has he changed his mind?"

It would be so easy to lie. To destroy the engagement with a bit of misdirection that resulted in an endless loop of he said, she said. But he had some honor. The decision to end it must be hers, Antonio's or theirs together.

"No. He's determined to see this through. He's very grateful to you."

She nodded as if his words affirmed something for her. "Thank you for your concern. There is much to adjust to, but I will honor my promise. In little over a month, I will marry Prince Antonio."

CHAPTER SIX

LINDSAY WAS STILL puzzling over what Zach felt compelled to talk to Christina about in private as she climbed to her room on the third floor of Hotel de la Calanetti, a lovely boutique hotel situated on a hillside overlooking Monte Calanetti's central courtyard.

Considering his opinion of lavish weddings and how unsettled Christina came across, leaving them alone together made Lindsay's left eyebrow tick. He better not have caused trouble.

In retrospect she wished she'd waited to say goodbye to Christina until after he'd spoken to her. Then Lindsay might have learned what the discussion had been about. Or maybe not. The other woman's natural poise hid a lot. Lindsay had been unable to tell if the woman was upset when she'd walked them out.

Holding the garment bag draped over her arm, Lindsay stepped aside so the hotel manager's teenage son, Mario, could unlock the door.

"Signorina." He ducked his head in a shy move and gestured for her to precede him.

She stepped in to a comfortable, refined room furnished with nice 1800s furniture. Thankfully there was a private bathroom. One large window allowed sunshine to flow in and provided a delightful view of the village and town center.

But it was tiny; smaller than the room at the farmhouse. Though this room included a desk, which she was happy to see, and a comfortable chair, she barely had space to walk around the double bed.

She tipped Mario—who'd lugged her suitcases up the three flights—with some change and a smile.

"Grazie, signorina." He rewarded her with a bashful grin and raced away.

The garment bag took up the entire closet to the point she had to bump it shut with her hip. She'd hoped to leave the dress with Christina, but the bride had nixed that plan. The queen had made a reservation with a favorite *modiste* in Milan and Christina had asked Lindsay to hold on to the dress and bring it to the fitting.

So of course that was what she'd do. And apparently everything else.

When Christina had walked them out, she'd given Lindsay a brief hug and whispered, "I trust you to finish it. Please make the prince proud."

Lindsay got the message. She was on her own for

the final push. Luckily her assistant would be arriving in a few days.

Hands on her hips Lindsay surveyed her room. It was lovely. And if she were here on vacation it would be perfect. But where was she going to work?

The desk for computer work was the least of her needs. She'd shipped five boxes of pre-wedding paraphernalia to the hotel. Upon check-in, Signora Eva had eagerly informed Lindsay the boxes had arrived and she'd be sending them up shortly.

Lindsay puffed out a breath that lifted her bangs. She thought longingly of the hillside villa Zach had pointed out as they'd flown over it. He had the whole place to himself. He probably had a room he could donate to the cause. Unfortunately he'd constantly be around. Talking to her. Distracting her. Tempting her.

Better to avoid that trap if she could.

She lifted her suitcase onto the bed and started unpacking. When she finished, she'd walk down to the town center to get a feel for the small city. She may have to find office space; possibly something off the town courtyard would be pleasant and close. In the meantime, she'd ask Signora Eva to hold on to the boxes.

Dressed in beige linen shorts and a cream, sleeveless tunic, Lindsay strolled down the hill. There was no sidewalk, just the ancient cobblestoned street. Charming but not the easiest to walk on.

A young man zipped by her on a scooter, followed closely by his female companion. Lindsay watched them until they turned a corner and vanished from view. She hadn't heard from the car-rental company yet. Monte Calanetti was a lovely little city, but not small enough she could do all her business by foot.

The zippy little scooter looked promising. It wouldn't hold anything, but she could have things delivered. But where? Not the hotel. She'd get claustrophobic after a day.

She reached the city center; not a courtyard, but a plaza. Oh, it was lovely. In the center an old fountain bubbled merrily, drawing Lindsay forward. Businesses ringed the plaza, many with hanging pots of flowers. It was bright and colorful and had probably looked much the same a hundred or even five hundred years ago.

Well, minus the cars, of course.

History in Tuscany wasn't something that needed to be brought to mind. The past surrounded you wherever you went, influenced your very thoughts. Already Lindsay was contemplating how she could make it a part of the wedding.

"Buon giorno, signorina," a male voice greeted her. "May I assist you in finding your way?"

She swung around to confront a large, barrel-chested man with a full head of black hair dusted gray on the sides. His bushy mustache was more gray than black. Friendly brown eyes waited patiently for her assessment.

"Hello." She smiled. "I'm just wandering." She waved her hand around. "I'm spellbound by the beauty of Monte Calanetti. You must be so proud the royal wedding will be performed here."

"Indeed we are. I am Alonso Costa, mayor of this fair city. I can assure you we have much to offer those who stay here. Amatucci's is one of the best boutique vineyards in the world, and Mancini's restaurant is superb. I fully expect Raffaele to earn an Italian Good Food Award this year. What is your interest, *signorina*? I will direct you to the best."

Oh, she was sure he could. She liked him instantly. He'd be a great source to help her.

"It's nice to meet you, Alonso, I'm Lindsay Reeves and I'd like to learn more about your beautiful city. Would you like to join me for coffee?"

White teeth flashed under the heavy bush of his mustache. "I would be most delighted, *signorina*. The café has a lovely cappuccino."

"Sounds wonderful." She allowed him to escort her across the plaza to an outdoor table at the café. He went inside and returned with two cappuccinos and some biscotti. She began to wonder if they had a gym in town. All this wonderful food, she'd be needing one soon.

She introduced herself more fully to the mayor and he proved a font of information. As she'd expected the media, both print and electronic, had already landed heavily in Monte Calanetti.

Alonso rubbed his chin when she asked after office space. "I will ask around. But I must warn you most available space has already been rented or reserved. The wedding has proved quite prosperous for the townspeople. Many have rented out spare rooms to house the paparazzi or provide work space as you have requested."

He named a figure a family had asked for the rental of their one-car garage and her mouth dropped open.

"Si," He nodded at her reaction. "It is crazy. But the press, they bid against each other to get the space."

"Well, it's more than I can afford. I'll have to figure out something else."

The empty chair next to Lindsay scraped back and Zach joined them at the table. He laid one arm along the back of her chair while holding his other hand out to Alonso. "Zach Sullivan. I've rented the De Luca villa."

"Ah, the best man." Alonso shook hands. "A palace representative provided a list of VIPs who would be visiting the area for the wedding. Your name is on the top."

Zach grinned. "It's good to know Tony has his priorities straight."

The casual reference to the prince impressed the mayor. He puffed up a bit as he gave Zach the same rundown about the town he'd given her. Except he offered to arrange a tour of the vineyard and make reservations at the restaurant. With great effort she restrained an eye roll.

"Tell me about the fountain," she asked to redirect the conversation.

Alonso gave her a bright smile. "The legend is that if you toss a coin and it lands in the clamshell you will get your wish. We recently learned that the sculptor of the nymph was Alberto Burano. The fact that the nymph wore a cloak caught the attention of an art historian. She recognized Burano's style and researched the fountain and Burano until she linked the two."

"That's amazing. And brings more value to the fountain and the city. Do you know anything more about the legend?"

"Actually, Lucia's search inspired me to do one of my own and I found that nymphs are known to be sensual creatures of nature, capricious in spirit living among humans but distant from them so when one presents an offering, such as the clamshell, it means the nymph has found true love and the offering is a gift of equal love."

"It's a lovely legend of unselfishness and love." The romance of it appealed to Lindsay.

"But does it work?" Zach questioned.

"Before I did the research I would have said half the time. Now, when I think back to the stories I've heard, success always involved matters of the heart. I believe when the coin lands in the clamshell it activates the gift and the wish is granted when true love is involved."

Zach quirked one dark eyebrow. "You're a romantic, Mr. Mayor."

Alonso smiled and shrugged in a very Italian gesture. "This is what I have observed. Does it make me a romantic to believe in the legend? Maybe so. But the tourists like it."

"I'm sure they do," Lindsay agreed. "Who doesn't like the thought of true love? Wouldn't it be cool to have a replica of the fountain at the reception?"

"*Si.* There is a mason in town that makes small replicas he sells to tourists. I'll give you his number. He might be able to make something bigger."

"That would be great. Thanks."

The mayor's cell phone rang. "Excuse me." He checked the display. "I must take this call. It has been a pleasure to meet you both. *Il caffè* is my treat today."

"Oh, no," Lindsay protested. "I invited you."

"And I am pleased you did. Allow me to welcome you both to Monte Calanetti with this small offering. You can reward me by thinking of local resources when planning this illustrious wedding."

"I already planned to do so."

"Ah—" he made a show of bowing over her hand "—a woman who is both beautiful and clever. You are obviously the right person for the job."

"You flatter me, Alonso. But I must be truthful. The bride insists that I use local goods and people whenever I can."

"Molto bene." He nodded, his expression proud. "Already our princess looks after the people. But I think maybe you would do this anyway, *si*?"

"I've found that local talent is often the best."

"Si, si. As I say, a clever woman. *Buona giornata.* Good day to you both. Ms. Reeves, I will get back to you with a referral. *Ciao.*" He made his exit, stopping to yell something inside the café. Then with a salute the mayor hurried across the square.

"I thought the French were supposed to be the flirts of Europe," Zach mused.

"I liked him."

"Of course. He was practically drooling over you. Clever woman."

She laughed and batted her lashes. "Don't forget beautiful."

His eyes locked on hers, the whiskey depths lit with heat. "How can I when you're sitting right next to me?"

Held captive by his gaze, by a quick and wicked

fantasy, it took a beat to compose herself. She cleared her throat as she chased the tail of the topic. Oh, yeah, the mayor. "You can tell he cares about his town and his people. I respect that. Excuse me."

She grabbed her purse and made her escape. Whew, the man was potent.

"Where are we going?" He slid into stride next to her.

And apparently hard to shake.

"*We* are not going anywhere." She reached the fountain and began to circle the stone feature, making the second answer unnecessary.

"I thought I made it clear, I'm here to assist you."

She flashed him a "yeah, right" glance.

"I appreciate the offer, but my assistant will be arriving at the end of the week." She continued circling.

"What are you doing?"

"I'm checking out the fountain, choosing the best place to throw a coin." The fountain was round, about twelve feet wide with a rock formation rising from slightly off center to a height between seven and eight feet. The cloaked nymph, reclined across two rocks from which the water flowed, reached forward, displaying one nude breast as she offered the clamshell to the side of the rushing water so some of it ran over the stone dish. If you threw too far to the left, the flow of water would wash your chance away, too far to the right and an over-cropping of rock would block the coin.

"You're going to make a wish? For true love? I thought your schedule didn't allow for such things."

"It doesn't." He was right about that. "It's not for me."

"For who then? Your mother?"

"Now there's a thought. But…no." Unfortunately she didn't know if her mother would recognize true love if she found it. She was so focused on the high, she rarely made it past the first few bumps. Even true love required an effort to make it work. "I'm making a wish for Antonio and Christina."

He stopped following her and planted his hands on his hips. "Why? They're already headed for the altar. They don't need the nymph's help."

"Really?" she challenged him. "You're that sure of them?"

His expression remained set. "I think fate should be allowed to take its course."

"And I think it needs a little help." She dug out her coin purse. Hopefully American coins worked as well as euros. Choosing a spot a little to the left because she was right-handed, she tossed her coin. Too light. It fell well short of the clamshell. She tried again. This one went over the top. A third got swept away by the water. "Dang it. That one was in."

"You're not going to make it in. It's set up to defeat you."

"Hey, no advice from the galley." Maybe a nickel? Oh, yeah, that had a nice heft. "What did you talk to Christina about earlier?"

"If I'd wanted you to know, I wouldn't have asked you to leave."

"Tell me anyway." The nickel bounced off the rock.

"No. Try a little twist at the end."

"I'd share with you," she pointed out as she tossed her last nickel. And missed.

"It's none of your business."

She fisted the dime she was about to throw and faced him. "Wrong. I'm here to plan the royal wedding, which makes the bride very much my business. She was already unsettled. And I know you're not a big fan of lavish weddings. I need to know if you upset her."

"I didn't upset her," he said too easily.

"Good. Great. So, tell me, what did you talk about?"

He just lifted a dark eyebrow at her.

"Seriously, I need to know. Just because she didn't look upset doesn't mean she wasn't."

"You're being a nutcase."

"And it'll all go away if you just tell me."

"Okay." He shoved his hands into his pockets. "I picked up on her uneasiness, as well. I asked her if she was having second thoughts."

"Zach!"

"What? This is my best friend. If she's going to bolt, now would be the time to speak up. Not when he's standing at the altar."

"I told you, all brides go through a bit of nerves. Unless you're the M-O-B, pointing out their shakiness only makes it worse. Even then it can be iffy."

His features went blank. "M-O-B?"

"Mother of the bride."

"Oh. She's probably the last person Christina would confide in."

"Why do you say that?"

"My impression is the two aren't particularly close."

"Hmm. Good to know." Lindsay had already noted Christina's reluctance to include her mother in the planning.

Mrs. Rose made her displeasure quite well known, which brought Mr. Rose out to play. Lucky for Lindsay the palace official had taken over dealing with the Roses.

"All the more reason to show Christina support rather than undermine her confidence," Lindsay advised Zach.

"Rest easy. She assured me she would be marrying Tony."

"Okay." She read his eyes and nodded. "Good. Thanks." She turned back to the fountain. "My last coin. What kind of twist?"

"You're still going to make a wish? I just told you Christina's fine."

"I want more than fine. I want true love."

"You do know most political marriages aren't based on love." Something in his tone had her swinging back to him. The late-afternoon sun slanted across his face, casting his grim features into light and shadow.

"Yes," she said softly, "but is that what you want for your friend?"

He moved closer, brushing her ponytail behind her shoulder. "So what is your wish?"

"I'm wishing for true love and happiness for the bride and groom." With the words, she pulled her arm back. As it moved forward Zach cupped her hand and, as she released the coin, gave it a little twist.

The dime flew through the air and plopped with a splash right in the middle of the clamshell.

"We did it!" Lindsay clapped her hands then threw her arms around Zach's neck and kissed his cheek. "Thank you."

He claimed a quick kiss then set her aside. "Don't celebrate yet. We still need to see if it works. Which should only take—what?—the next fifty years."

"Nope." Flustered from the kiss, Lindsay stepped back shifting her attention from him to the fountain. What had he said? Oh, yeah. How did it work? "Now we have faith."

* * *

The first attempt to find the brooch was a bust.

Lindsay tried insisting she could handle finding the brooch herself. It was something she could do while she waited for her assistant to arrive and figured out her work space situation. And she needed a break from Zach, especially after the kiss at the fountain. His casual caresses were becoming too common and were definitely too distracting for her peace of mind.

A little distance between them would be a good thing.

Unfortunately, as he pointed out, Christina's grandmother lived in a tiny house in a village halfway between Monte Calanetti and Voti, and Lindsay didn't have transportation without him. A new rental hadn't showed up and the helicopter flew at his discretion. Plus, he'd offered to interpret for her. Since Mona didn't speak much English and Lindsay didn't speak much Italian, she was stuck.

Mona Rose was small with white hair, glasses and lots of pip. She greeted them warmly as Christina had called to say they would be coming. Lindsay sat on a floral-print couch with crocheted lace doilies on the arms while Zach lounged in a matching rocking chair.

Mona served them hibiscus tea and lemon cake while she chatted with Zach.

Lindsay smiled and sipped. After a few minutes of listening, she discreetly kicked Zach in the foot.

He promptly got the clue. "She's very pleased Christina wishes to wear the brooch. She wore the brooch for her wedding and had many happy years with her Benito. Her daughter, Cira, chose not to wear the brooch and now she's divorced with two children."

"I'm sorry to hear that." Lindsay accepted a plate of cake. "Does she know where the brooch is?"

Zach conveyed the question.

Mona tapped her chin as she stared out the window. After a moment she took a sip of her tea and spoke. "Sophia, my youngest sister, I think was last to wear *le broccia*." She shook her head and switched to Italian.

Zach translated. "Pia is her older sister. Her daughter was the last to get married. She didn't wear the brooch, either, but Mona thinks Pia may have it."

"Grazie." Lindsay directed her comments to Mona, smiling to hide her disappointment. She was hoping this chore could be done.

"Would you be willing to do a quick look through your things while we're here? Just to be on the safe side."

Zach translated both the question and Mona's answer.

"Si. I will look. Christina is a good girl. And Antonio, he is good for Halencia. But they will both need much luck."

* * *

The next morning Lindsay struggled to get ready while shuffling around five large boxes. When she'd returned to the hotel last night, all five boxes had been delivered to her room. As predicted, she'd had a hard time getting around the bed. She'd actually had to climb over it to get to the bathroom.

When she'd asked about it at the front desk, Signora Eva apologized but explained a delivery of provisions had forced her to reclaim the space she'd been using to store Lindsay's boxes. That had meant the boxes needed to be delivered to Lindsay's room. This morning she'd managed to arrange them so she had a small aisle around the bed, but she had to suck in a breath to get through.

The thought of unpacking everything in this limited space made her cringe. She'd be tripping over her samples every time she turned around.

Frustrated, she left the room for some breakfast. Later she wanted to view the palazzo and chapel where the wedding and reception would take place. But she hoped to rent a scooter before making the trip to the other side of town.

If any were still available.

The press truly had descended. On her way to breakfast she fended off two requests for exclusive shots of the wedding dress. She informed them the dress was under lock and key at the palace and suffered no remorse for her lie.

When Signora Eva came by to refill her coffee, Lindsay asked if she knew of any place she might rent for a work space and received much the same response as she'd gotten from the mayor.

She was processing that news when her cell rang.

With a sinking heart she listened to her assistant advise her she wouldn't be joining her in Halencia, after all. While Mary gushed on about the part she'd landed in a situation comedy all Lindsay could think about was how she'd manage without an assistant.

Lindsay needed to be out in the field a lot. She counted on her assistant to keep track of all the details of a wedding, do follow up and advise Lindsay of any problems. She'd quickly become bogged down if she had to take on the extra work.

Because she cared about Mary, Lindsay mustered the enthusiasm to wish her well. But as soon as she hung up she had a mini meltdown. Stomping over to the sideboard, she plopped an oversize muffin onto her plate and returned to her seat, her mind churning over her lack of options...

As Lindsay made the hike up the hill to Zach's villa she contemplated the obvious answer to her space problem. Much as she preferred to avoid Zach, after two short days she seriously considered asking him for help.

Her hesitation wasn't worry over his answer. He'd been ordered to assist her and he genuinely seemed to take his duty seriously.

The problem would be in dealing with him.

From the air, the villa had looked vast enough to provide a small corner for her without causing her to trip over him at every turn. But she wouldn't know until she saw the inside, which is what had prompted this little trip.

She wiped her brow with the back of her hand. Only eight in the morning and already the day had some heat to it. The blue, cloudless sky offered little relief from the relentless sun. But it also meant no humidity.

"Good morning, partner." Zach's voice floated on the air.

She paused and shaded her eyes to seek him out. He stood on a terrace of his rented villa. The big, stone building rested right up against the old protective wall that ringed the city. From this vantage point it looked huge. Three stories high, the bottom floor created the terrace where Zach stood. The top floor was a pergola with windows on all sides.

"Good morning." She waved.

"You missed the street." He gestured for her to backtrack a bit. "It's a narrow drive right by the pink house."

She followed his directions, turning at the pink house, and there he was coming to greet her. He wore khaki shorts and a blue cotton shirt untucked. The sleeves were rolled to expose his muscular forearms. He looked cool, calm and competent.

How she envied him.

The trees thinned as they neared the villa. He took her hand and led her down a steep set of steps and a walkway along the side of the house. When they rounded the corner, her breath caught in her throat.

The small city spread out below them, a backdrop to the green lawn that covered the hillside. Oak, olive and pine trees provided shade and privacy. To her right a table and chairs sat under a covered patio, the ivy-covered trellis lending it a grotto effect while a stone path led to a gazebo housing white wicker furniture.

To the far side rosebushes lined a path leading to an infinity pool.

Forget the palazzo. This would make a beautiful setting for a wedding. Well, if you weren't a royal prince.

She took pride in the large, lavish weddings she'd planned for hip and rising celebrities, but she took joy in putting together weddings that were cozy gatherings. Yup, give her intimate and tranquil over pomp and circumstance any day of the week.

"Come up with me." A spiral wrought-iron staircase took them to the terrace he'd been standing on when he'd hailed her. She followed his tight butt up the steps.

Good dog, he was fine. His body rivaled any sight

she'd seen today. Even the view from the terrace that provided a panoramic vista of everything she'd seen.

"Impressed yet?" Zach asked behind her left ear.

"I passed impressed before I reached the pool."

"I had my coffee out here this morning. I don't think I've ever spent a more peaceful moment."

"I'm jealous." She stepped away from the heat of his body. She needed her wits about her when she presented her proposition. His assertion they'd be lovers haunted her thoughts. And dreams.

Oh, she was a weak, weak woman in her dreams.

As heat flooded her cheeks she focused on the view rather than his features. "I'm afraid I'm about to disrupt your peace."

"Pixie, just looking at you disrupts my peace. In the best possible way." He punctuated the remark by tracing the armhole of her sleeveless peach-and-white polka dot shirt, the backs of his fingers feathering over sensitive flesh.

She shivered, shaking a finger at him as she created distance between them. "No touching."

He grinned, again unrepentant. "What brings you by today?"

"I wondered if you wanted to go to the cake tasting with me." She tossed out her excuse for the spy mission. Men liked cake, right?

As soon as the words left her mouth, she thought better of her desperate plan. If she worked here, it would be more of his charming flirtation and subtle caresses until she gave in and let him have his wicked way with her. Or she stopped the madness by seducing him on the double lounge down by the pool. Enticing as both scenarios were, neither was acceptable.

"You know…never mind. I've already taken advantage of your generosity. Enjoy your peace. I can handle this on my own." She turned for the stairs. "I'll catch you later."

The chemistry between them nearly struck sparks in the air. The force of the pull buzzed over her skin like a low-level electrical current. She had it banked at the moment, but the right word or look and it would flare to life in a heartbeat.

Her best bet was to walk away and find another solution to her problem. One that didn't tempt her to break her sensible rules and put her company at risk. She purposely brought Kevin to mind, remembered the pain and humiliation of his betrayal and recalled the looks of pity and disapproval on the faces of her friends and colleagues.

She'd never willingly put herself in that position ever again.

"Cake." Zach caught her gently by the elbow. "You can't tease me with cake and then walk away. It's one of the few chores regarding this wedding gig I'd actually enjoy."

She studied him for a moment before replying. He met her stare straight-on, no hint of flirting in his steady regard. She appreciated his sincerity but still she hesitated.

"Okay. You're in. But we have to go now. I have an appointment to view the palazzo this afternoon. Has the rental company replaced your car yet?"

"No. I have my assistant following up on it. Do we need the helicopter?"

She shook her head. "The bakery is in town." She supposed she'd have to follow up on her own rental now. Pulling out her phone, she made a note. "But it's hot out. My plan is to rent a scooter."

A big grin brought out a boyishness in his features. "You don't have to rent a scooter. There are a couple downstairs in the garage along with something else you might find useful."

"What?"

"Come see." He strode over to a French door and stepped inside.

Trailing behind him, she admired the interior almost as much as the exterior. The bedroom they moved through displayed the comfort and luxury of a five-star hotel. Downstairs it became apparent the villa had gone through a modern update. The lounge, dining room and gourmet kitchen opened onto each other via large archways, creating an open-concept format while exposed beams and stone floors retained the old world charm of a Tuscan villa.

Oh, yeah, she could work here. Too bad it was a no-go.

Off the kitchen Zach opened a door and went down a half flight of stairs to the garage. He flipped a light and she grinned at what she saw. A sporty black golf cart with a large cargo box in the back filled half the space. On the far side were two red scooters.

"Sweet. This will work nicely."

"Dibs on the cart."

She lifted her eyebrows at him. "What are you, ten?"

"No, I'm six-four. I'd look foolish trying to ride the scooter."

Running her gaze over the full length of him, she admired the subtle muscles and sheer brawn of his wide shoulders. She saw his point. He'd look as though he were riding a child's toy.

He grunted. "Work with me here, Lindsay. You can't tell me no touching and then look at me like that."

"Sorry," she muttered. She claimed the passenger seat. Caught.

Turned out wedding planning could be quite tasty. Zach finished the last bite of his sample of the white amaretto cake with the vanilla bean buttercream icing. And way more complicated than it needed to be.

The baker, a reed-thin woman with a big smile

and tired eyes, had six samples set out for them when they'd arrived at the quaint little shop on a cobblestoned street just off the plaza. She'd dusted her hands on her pink ruffled apron and explained what each sample was.

Lindsay explained Christina had already chosen the style and colors for the cake; their job was to pick out the flavors for the three different layers. It took him five minutes to pick his three favorites. Lindsay agreed with two but not the third. He was happy to let her have her preference, but…no. The baker brought out six more samples, which were all acceptable.

The fact was they couldn't go wrong whatever choice they made. There was no reason this appointment needed to be an hour long. But Lindsay insisted the flavors be compatible.

They were finally done and he was finishing off the samples of his favorites while Lindsay completed the order with the baker up at the counter.

He'd be taking a back seat on the hands-on stuff from now on. He was a stickler for attention to detail, but efficiency had its place, too.

The little bell over the door rang as two men strolled in, one tall and bald, the other round and brown-haired. They eyed the goods on display and Zach heard a British slant to their accent.

He knew immediately when they realized who Lindsay was. They closed in on her, obviously trying to see the plans for the cake. Their interest marked them as two of the media horde invading the town.

Lindsay politely asked them to step back.

Baldy moved back a few inches but Brownie made no move to honor her request.

Zach's gaze narrowed on the two, waiting to see how Lindsay handled herself. His little pixie had a feisty side. She wouldn't appreciate his interference. And this may well blow over. All press weren't bad, but he knew money could make people do things they'd never usually contemplate.

Ignoring the looming goons, Lindsay wrapped up her business and turned toward him. The media brigade blocked her exit, demanding details about the cake, pestering her for pictures. She tried to push past them but they went shoulder to shoulder, hemming her in.

In an instant Zach crossed the room.

"You're going to want to let her by."

"Wait your turn." Brownie dismissed him. "Come on, sweetcakes, show us something."

Sweetcakes?

"It's always my turn." Zach placed a hand on either man's shoulder and shoved them apart.

They whirled on him like a mismatched tag team.

"Back up," Brownie snarled at Zach's chest. And then he slowly lifted his gaze to Zach's. Even Baldy had to look up.

Zach rolled his thick shoulders. That's all it usually took. Sure enough, both men took a large step back.

"Ms. Reeves is with me." He infused the quiet words with a bite of menace. "I won't be pleased if I see you bothering her again."

"Hey, no disrespect." Baldy quickly made his exit. Brownie clenched his jaw and slowly followed.

"Thank you." Lindsay appeared at his side. "Those two were more aggressive than most."

"Are you okay?" He pulled her into his arms. "Do you put up with that often?" He couldn't tolerate the thought of her being hassled by those media thugs on her own.

"All the time." For a moment she stood stiffly, but with a sigh she melted against him. "One of the guys at my hotel offered me a hundred-thousand dollars for a picture of the wedding dress, which means the tabloids are probably willing to pay a million for it."

"That explains why you've lugged it halfway across the world."

"I said it was locked up at the palace. But for a million dollars, I don't doubt someone might try to check out my room anyway."

That did it. He may not support this wedding, but he had his limits. He wouldn't put his plan, or Tony's happiness, before Lindsay's safety. The thought of her vulnerable on her own at the hotel and someone forcing their way into her room sent a primitive wave of rage blasting through him. He had to fix this.

"You should give up your room at the hotel and stay with me at the villa. It would be safer for you."

CHAPTER SEVEN

"UH, NO." LINDSAY pushed away from the safety of his arms. Yes, she'd been spooked by the menacing media jerks, but was Zach totally insane? "That is not an option." She even thought better of asking for work space at the villa. "This—" she waved between the two of them, indicating the chemistry they shared "—makes it a bad idea."

"Even I'm picking up on what a big deal this is for the press." He led her back to their table. "It didn't really strike me at first. I'm used to photographers hanging around hawking at Antonio for a picture. Some of them can be unscrupulous in their bid for a shot." He sat back crossing his arms over his chest his gaze intent, focused on her, on the problem. She had a sudden, clear vision of what he'd look like sitting at his desk. "It's the only solution that makes sense."

She sent him a droll stare. "You're just saying that to get in my pants."

"Not so."

The bite in the denial sent embarrassed heat rushing through her.

"Yes, I want in your pants, but not at the expense of your safety."

She blinked at him, her emotions taking a moment to catch up with her hearing. Obviously she'd touched a nerve.

"Okay."

"Excellent." Satisfied, he leaned forward in his chair. "It's settled. You'll move into the villa. We'll find a secure spot for the dress and you can choose a room for yourself and one of the spare rooms for your office. Or you can use the sunroom if you prefer."

"No. Wait." Panicked, she made a sharp cut-off gesture with her hand. "I was acknowledging your comment not agreeing to move in. We need to talk about this."

"We just did."

"Yes, and I appreciate your putting my safety ahead of your libido, but what does that mean? I've told you how I feel about maintaining a professional distance with all members of the wedding party, especially the best man."

A raised eyebrow mocked her. "I remember."

She gritted her teeth. "Well, you're a touchy-feely guy and I can't deal with that in a professional relationship."

A stunned expression flashed across his well-defined features but was quickly replaced with a contemplative mask.

"You have my promise I'll try to keep my hands to myself."

"The problem with that sentence is the word *try*."

He ran a hand over the back of his neck, kneading the muscles and nerves as if to relieve tension, studying her the whole time. Then he flexed his shoulders and faced her.

"Here's the deal. I'm not a touchy-feely guy. Not normally. I go after what I want, but I respect boundaries and I can handle being told no."

Yeah, like that happened.

"For some reason it's different with you. I like my hands on you, like the touch and taste of you to the degree it's instinctive to seek it."

OMD. That is so hot.

"So, yes. I promise to *try*."

She gulped. "Okay."

His eyes flashed dark fire. "Is that okay you'll stay or—"

"Yes. Okay, I'll move in." It may be insane to move in with him, but she would feel safer. Plus, it solved her work problem. "But I'm keeping my room at the hotel. Space is already at a premium here in Monte Calanetti and I need a place I can retr—uh…go to if things don't work out."

"Fair enough. And as a gesture of my commitment, I'll pay for the room since you won't be using it."

"That's not necessary."

"It is to me. I'll feel better with you at the villa, and I want you to know you can trust me."

She slowly nodded. "Okay. I'll go pack."

"I had your boxes delivered up here, but if you choose this space, you'll need a proper desk. It has a bar and a billiard table, but that's it."

"I don't need anything new," Lindsay protested.

"I doubt the owners will object to us leaving behind an extra piece of furniture."

"That's not the point." He'd warned her that the space lacked a desk or table for her laptop. But, seriously, she didn't see the problem; she sat with it in her lap half the time.

"Pixie." He stopped in the upper hallway and swung to face her. His hand lifted to touch but he caught himself and curled the fingers into a fist that he let drop to his side. "Didn't you look at the numbers? The government contract will lift me to billionaire status. I can afford a desk."

He opened a door she'd thought was a linen closet. It revealed a staircase of stone steps. His hand gestured for her go ahead of him.

"First of all—" she paused in front of him "—congratulations."

A pleased smile lit his eyes. The simple expression of joy made her glad she'd put that first.

She got the feeling he received very little positive reinforcement in his personal life. The business world recognized and respected his genius, and his employees obviously appreciated his success and most likely his work ethic. But as an only child whose parents ignored his personal business interests in favor of their own agenda for him to join his father in politics, who did he have that mattered to tell him job well done?

She shook the thought away. He was not a poor, unfortunate child, but an intelligent, successful man.

And he'd hate her pity.

"Second—" she started up the stairs "—it's not for you to buy me a desk."

"The duties of a best man are unlimited. But you could be right. Do you want me to call Tony and ask him? Because I can pretty much guarantee his response will be, 'If the wedding planner needs a desk then buy her a desk. And don't bother me with such trivial things.'"

Aggrieved, she rolled her eyes, making sure he saw as she rounded the bend in the stairs. "Please, even if he blew off the request that easily, he wouldn't add that last bit."

"Not only would he say it, Pixie, that was the clean version. Tony doesn't have a whole lot of patience these days."

"He must be dealing with a lot—oh, I love, love, *love* this."

She strolled into the middle of the bright room

and did a slow turn. The room was a long octagon. Three walls were made of glass and windows, two others were of stone and one held a fireplace. The last was half stone, the other half was a stained-glass mural of a Tuscan hillside; a bar with brown-cushioned stools ran almost the full length of the wall. At the far end there was a door. She checked it out and found it opened onto another spiral staircase that led to the terrace below.

"A separate entrance."

"Yes, I'll give you a set of keys. When your assistant gets here, she can still have access if we're gone."

"That'd be great but my assistant won't be coming."

"What happened?"

"My practical, poised, ever-efficient assistant finally landed a part in a sitcom."

"Ah, the joy of proprietorship in Hollywood."

Still feeling deserted, Lindsay nodded. "It's the third time it's happened to me. Of course, I'm thrilled for her. But seriously? Worst timing ever."

"Hey, listen. I'm the first to admit this wedding stuff is not my thing, but I'll help where I can."

"Thanks, but you've done enough by offering me this space. I'll finally be able to put up my wedding board. And the help I need involves a hundred little things, well below your pay grade." She really couldn't see him playing secretary. And she may appreciate the space and assistance, but the last thing she needed was to have him constantly underfoot.

"There's no help for it. I'll have to hire someone local. Maybe Alonso knows someone he can recommend. On the plus side, it will be good to have someone who knows the area and the people, who speaks the language and knows the cost of things."

"Alonso will know someone. In the meantime, I'm sticking with you. I'll get a locksmith in to reinforce the locks on all the doors."

She wanted to protest the need for him to shadow her. Instead she nodded, knowing he was reacting out of concern for her. And she was happy to have the extra security for the dress. It might seem a bother for something they'd only have for another week, but she'd be more comfortable knowing the villa was secure.

She strolled further into the room. In soft beige and sage green, the furniture looked sturdy and comfortable. A U-shaped couch invited her to sit and enjoy the amazing view. The billiard table Zach had mentioned was on the right and her boxes were stacked on the green felt. Past it was the fireplace wall with a bookshelf that offered a wide selection of reading material. Another door hid a bathroom.

The ceiling was high, the beams exposed, and a large fan circulated the air in the room.

There were only two low-slung tables. One in

front of the large couch and one between the swivel chairs near the fireplace.

"Oh, yeah, I can work here. No hardship at all." She'd totally make do.

Hands on his hips, Zach surveyed the room. "You'll need a desk." He repeated his earlier decree. "And you mentioned a wedding board. Is that a whiteboard?"

"A whiteboard would be nice, too. My wedding board is usually a corkboard. I need to be able to tack things to it."

He had his phone in his hands and was making notes. She sighed, knowing there'd be no shaking him until she hired an assistant. In one sense it was reassuring to know she wasn't on her own, but it made her plan to avoid him a no-go. It was almost as if fate were working against her.

"I guess we have our shopping list, then. What do you want to do now? Unpack your boxes? You said earlier that you wanted to check out the palazzo."

"Yes. The boxes can wait." Better to have the boards when she went to do that, anyway. "But, honestly, there's no need for you to accompany me. Stay. Enjoy your day."

"I'm coming with you."

Of course he was. At this point, it was easier to agree than to argue. "Fine. Let me call Louisa and remind her I'm coming then we can go."

"Who's Louisa?"

"The owner of the palazzo. We've spoken a couple of times. She seems nice. Did you hear they discovered a fresco when they were restoring the chapel?"

"No. That's quite a discovery. It has to add to the property value."

"You are such a guy."

"Pixie, were you in any doubt?"

"Hello, Louisa, it's so nice to finally meet you. Thank you for allowing us to tour the property today." Lindsay greeted the owner of the palazzo.

It surprised Zach to see Louisa was an American. The two women were close to the same age but dissimilar in every other way. Louisa topped Lindsay by four or five inches and wore her white-blond hair in a messy knot on top of her head. Her willowy frame and restrained posture gave her a brittle appearance.

Funny, she held no attraction for him because she fit his type to a tee: long, lithe, and blond. Sure he recognized she was a beautiful woman, but she appeared almost fragile next Lindsay's vibrancy.

"Louisa, I have to say I'm a little concerned. I thought the renovation would be further along." Lindsay swept her hand out to indicate the overgrown vegetation and construction paraphernalia strewed through the courtyard and surrounding grounds.

"I can see why you'd be confused." Louisa's smile was composed. "But we're actually right on schedule. They've just completed the interior restoration. The construction crew will be back today to finish clearing out their equipment and trash. The next step is the landscapers, but I was actually thinking of hiring some men from town first, to just clear all this out."

"That might be a good idea," Lindsay agreed. "Just level it and start fresh."

"Exactly. I can see some rosebushes, lavender and a few wild sunflowers. But it's so overgrown it's hard to know if they'd be worth saving if we took the time and effort to clear the weeds around them."

Lindsay nodded as the other woman talked. "I think you have the right idea."

Zach enjoyed watching them interact. He liked how Lindsay's ponytail bobbed as she talked and the way the sunshine picked up golden highlights in her hair.

He almost forgot his purpose in shadowing her every move.

Mostly because it was against his nature to be covert, to be less than helpful. Case in point: this morning. When he saw Lindsay being intimidated by the press, he jumped right into fix-it mode and invited her to move into the spacious villa. And he'd provided her with a prime workspace. Hell, he fully intended to get her a desk.

All of which went against his prime objective of keeping Antonio from a life of misery. With that thought Zach took out his phone and texted his friend, tagging him for a meeting time.

Right now his biggest problem was the blurring line between his mock flirtation with Lindsay and his honest reactions. There'd been too much truth in his arguments to get her to stay at the villa. She was too comfortable to be around, too soft to the touch, too easy to imagine in his bed.

And too dangerous to succumb to.

He hadn't felt this way about a woman since… ever. And he wasn't going there.

From here on out he was back on his game.

"Thanks for talking it through with me." Louisa folded her arms in front of her. "I'm very grateful to the monarchy for doing the renovation of the palazzo and chapel. I certainly couldn't have afforded anything this elaborate all at once. Probably never, come to that. But it's been a pretty intense process. It's good to have someone to discuss a decision with."

"I bet." Lindsay grinned. "Call on me anytime. I'm great at discussion."

"I can see you are." A friendly sparkle entered Louisa's light blue eyes. "And probably pretty good at decisions, too."

Lindsay rocked on her heals. "Yeah, it's kind of part of the job description."

The composed smile held a little more warmth as Louisa gestured to the chapel. "Shall we do a walk-through? I'm afraid we'll have to make this fairly quick. I have an appointment in Florence tomorrow. I'm driving over tonight so I'll be there in the morning. I've booked passage on the two o'clock ferry."

"That's fine. Today I just want to get a feel for the place and take some pictures so I know what I'm working with. And—oh, this is beautiful." Lindsay surveyed the interior of the chapel with a mix of wonder and calculation on her face. "So charming with the arched windows and the dark wood pews. I can come back on another day to get actual measurements and check out the lighting. I love how the jewel colors flow over the stone tiles from the stained-glass windows. Christina has chosen an afternoon wedding and evening reception. She wants to have it outdoors, so the landscaping will be important."

"I won't be able to hire the workers to clear the grounds until I return from Florence," Louisa informed her, "but I'll make it a priority when I get back."

"Why don't I handle that for you?" Zach offered, seeing an opportunity to cause a few days' delay. He'd simply tell the workers to be careful to preserve any original flowers. "I'll talk to the mayor to get some referrals."

"Thank you. I appreciate it. They did a wonderful

job with the restoration," Louisa stated. "It was quite a mess in here. Stones were missing, the stained-glass windows were broken and some of the walls had wood covering them. Here's the fresco that was uncovered." Louisa moved to a shallow alcove and Zach followed Lindsay over.

He understood her gasp. The ancient painting of Madonna and child took his breath away. The colors were vibrant, the detail exquisite. It was almost magnetic—the pull of the fresco, from the pinky tones of Jesus's skin and the color of Mary's dark blue robe, to the white and yellow of the brilliant beam of light encasing them and the greens of the surrounding countryside bright with orange and red flowers. The details were so exact, every brush stroke so evident, it seemed it could have been painted a week ago rather than five hundred years.

"Look at the love on their faces." Lindsay breathed. "The artist caught the perfect expression of Mary's unconditional love for her child and Baby Jesus's childlike wonder and awe for his mother. It shows the full bond between mother and child. This will certainly add to the ambience of the wedding."

With the beauty and love inherent in the fresco, Zach could see how she'd think so. But with his friend's future and happiness at risk, he couldn't take that chance.

Zach surprised Lindsay with his patience and insight the next day as they toured four nurseries. She had a whole list of requirements from bouquets and boutonnieres to centerpieces and garlands and more.

Lindsay planned to use roses for the groomsmen, sunflowers over linen chair covers for the reception and a combination of the two for everything else.

To bring about a sense of intimacy in the courtyard and to define the separate areas for eating and dancing, she planned to have rustic scaffolding erected. Lights, flowers and silk drapery would blend rustic with elegance to create a sense of old and new. She actually appreciated Zach's male point of view and his logistical input.

The helicopter came in handy as they buzzed around the countryside. Deciding on the second vendor she spoke with, Lindsay asked to return to the nursery to put in her order. Zach made no argument. He simply directed the pilot and helped her aboard.

Zach waited patiently in an anteroom of the magnificent palace. He stood at the terrace doors overlooking a section of the rose garden. Curved benches spaced several feet apart created a circle around a marble fountain of a Roman goddess.

Lindsay would love it. He had to hand it to her, that woman worked. He could practically hear her discourse on what a lovely venue the rose garden would be for a wedding, how the circle represented the ring and the ring represented the commitment made between bride and groom, who once joined together there became no beginning and no end, just the unity of their bond.

"Yeah, right."

"Talking to yourself, *amico mio*?" a gruff voice said before a hand clapped on his shoulder.

"Just keeping myself company waiting for you."

"I'm glad you came." Tony pulled Zach into the hug he'd learned to endure through the years. Tony was a demonstrative man, how could he not be with such passionate parents?

"Yeah, well, it became clear if I wanted to see you, I'd have to come to you."

"I only have thirty minutes. I wish I had more time to give you. Hell, I wish we were at Clancy's eating wings, drinking beer and catching a game."

"We could be there in fourteen hours," Zach said, hoping it would be that easy.

Tony laughed. "I'm tempted." He opened the terrace door and stepped outside. To the left stood a table with comfortable chairs. And a bucket of beers on ice.

"What, no chicken wings?"

"They are on the way."

Zach sat across from his friend and leaned back in his chair. Tony looked tired. And harassed. Zach knew Tony had to be busy for him to put Zach off. They were as close as brothers, too close for the other man to brush him aside.

"How are things going with the wedding?" Tony asked.

"Let's just say I could tell you in excruciating detail and leave it at that."

Tony grinned. "Thanks, bro. I mean that."

"Only for you," Zach assured him. "How are things going here?"

"Slowly." Tony grabbed a beer and opened it. "Everyone has a different opinion of how the monarchy should be run."

"And you have to learn the worst-case scenario for each before you'll make a determination," Zach stated, knowing that's how his friend operated. In working security protocols he liked to work backward to make sure the worst never happened.

"It doesn't help that I constantly have to address some question or concern about the wedding or coronation. It's a lot to juggle."

"So maybe you should put the wedding off." Zach took the opportunity presented to him. "Get the monarchy stabilized first and then revisit the idea of marriage when you can choose someone for yourself."

"Are you kidding me?" Tony laughed again. "Instead of cheering me, the people would be rioting in the streets. I think they want this wedding more than anything else."

"Because it's a Cinderella story?"

Tony shrugged. "Because I've made them wait so long."

"Because you never intended to marry Christina."

"Shush." Tony glanced around the terrace. "We won't speak of that here."

"Someone needs to speak of it before it's too late to stop it."

"That time is long gone, my friend. Christina will make a good queen. The people love her."

"They don't know her any better than you do. She's been off in Africa."

"Taking care of sick children. It plays well. Ah, the chicken wings. *Grazie*, Edmondo."

The servant bowed and retreated.

Zach quirked a brow at his friend. Tony shrugged and they both reached for a chicken wing.

After a moment Tony sighed. "Man, I needed this." He upended his beer, drinking the last. "I don't know anything about running a country, Zach."

"You know plenty. You've been training for this your whole life. Even while living in California," Zach reminded him.

"That's different. I always planned to hand over control to a republic, but I'm not sure that's what the people want. They are all behind this wedding and I can't let them down. I just need to do the opposite of what my dad would do and I'll be doing a better job than has been done."

"A little harsh, don't you think?"

"No." Tony shook his head and reached for another beer. "I love my parents, but their relationship is messed up. I don't ever want to love anyone so much it messes with my head. Better a business arrangement than a volatile, emotional mess."

Zach plucked a bottle of beer from the bucket, knowing he'd gotten as far as he was going to get tonight. He reached out and clicked bottles with Tony. "To the monarchy."

Tony's statement about a business arrangement only made Zach more determined to see him freed from a loveless marriage. Because his friend was wrong. At least a volatile, emotional mess inferred someone cared. You didn't get that guarantee with a business arrangement. What you got was a cold, lonely life.

CHAPTER EIGHT

WHAT A DIFFERENCE a week made. As she flew through the air on the way to Milan, Lindsay thought about all she'd accomplished since her last flight in the helicopter. She had her wedding board up and she'd made contact with all the local vendors she'd lined up before coming to Halencia, confirming plans and reevaluating as necessary.

She'd talked to the landscapers and she had an appointment at the end of the week to meet at the palazzo to go over her needs for the wedding and reception. On the mayor's recommendation, Zach had hired a crew to clean up the palazzo and chapel grounds. They should be well done by the time she met with the landscapers.

Yesterday she'd hired an assistant. Serena was twenty-two, fresh out of university and eager to assist in any way she could with the royal wedding. Lindsay worried a little over the girl's age, knowing she'd have to be strong enough to say no to outrageous offers for inside information about the wedding, and mature enough to know when she was being played. But Serena was Mayor Alonso's daughter and she had his glib tongue and a no-nonsense attitude that convinced Lindsay she could handle the job.

Plus, she just plain liked the young woman.

She'd gone a little googly-eyed over Zach but, seriously, who wouldn't? It was a fact of life she'd have to put up with.

"We are coming up on Milano," the pilot announced.

Lindsay leaned forward to get a view of the northern city. Two prominent pieces of architecture caught the eye. A very modern building of glass and metal that twisted well into the air and an ancient cathedral dramatically topped with a forest of spires. Both buildings were stunningly impressive.

She glanced at Zach and found his gaze on her. Smiling, she gestured at the view. "It's spectacular."

"It is, indeed," he agreed without looking away from her.

She turned her attention back to the view, pretending his focus on her didn't send the blood rushing through her veins.

He'd kept to his promise not to touch her. Well, mostly. He didn't play with her hair or take her hand, but he stayed bumping-elbows close wherever they went. And he still liked to put his hand in the small of her back whenever he directed her into or out of a building or room.

Serena had asked if they were together, so Lindsay knew the townspeople were speculating about their relationship. She'd given Serena a firm no in response and hoped the word got out about the true state of things.

They landed at a heliport on a mid-rise building not far from the Duomo di Milano. Downstairs a car was waiting to take them to a shop along Via Monte Napoleone. Lindsay checked her tablet to give Zach the address.

She looked forward to handing the dress over to Christina and the queen's seamstress. Providing security for the gown had proved more stressful than she'd anticipated. Having it off her shoulders would allow her to focus on the many other elements of the wedding demanding her attention.

"There it is. Signora Russo's. Christina and the queen are meeting us there. I already spoke to Signora Russo about the damage to the beading. She said she's a master seamstress and she would fix it."

"I'm glad to hear it."

A valet took the car and she and Zach were escorted inside. An attendant took the garment bag and led them to a plush fitting suite. A large, round couch in a soft ivory with a high back topped by an extravagant flower arrangement graced the middle of the room.

The bride and queen stood speaking with a petite, ageless woman in a stylish black suit. Lindsay walked across the room with Zach to join them.

Christina made the introductions. It might have been Lindsay's imagination, but the other woman seemed quite relieved to see them.

"Zachary!" exclaimed Her Royal Highness Valentina de l'Accardi, Queen of Halencia when she saw Zach. "As handsome as ever." She glided forward and kissed him on both cheeks. "*Mio caro*, thank you for helping Antonio. He is so busy. Many, many meetings. We do not even see him at the palace."

"Valentina." Zach bent over her hand. "You are ever youthful. I thought for a moment Elena was here."

"Zachary!" Valentina swatted his forearm and giggled. Yes, the matriarch of Halencia giggled. And flushed a pretty rose. "Such a charming boy. Be careful, Ms. Reeves, this one knows what a woman wants to hear, be alert that he does not steal your heart."

"Yes. I've noticed he's a bit of a flirt."

"*Si*, a flirt." Warm brown eyes met hers with a seriousness her lighthearted greeting belied. The woman clasped her hand and patted it. "I am so pleased you were able to come to Halencia to plan Antonio and Christina's wedding. I wanted only the best for them."

"Now, you flatter me." Lindsay squeezed the

queen's hand before releasing her and stepping back. "It is I who is privileged to be here. And to be here in Signora Russo's shop. I may have to steal a moment to shop for my own dress for the wedding."

"Oh, you must. My friend will take the best care of you. Giana, Ms. Reeves needs a dress. Charge it to my account. It shall be my treat for all her hard work."

Appalled, Lindsay protested. "Your Highness, I cannot—"

"I insist." The queen waved her objection aside. "I only wish I could stay and help you shop. And see Christina in her gown!" She sighed with much drama. "Regretfully, I must leave. One of Antonio's many meetings draws me away. Christina—" Valentina moved to the bride's side and Christina bowed to receive a kiss on the cheek. "Worry not. Giana has made many women look like a princess. She will do her *magia* and make you a *bella* bride."

For an instant Christina seemed to freeze, but in a blink it passed and she bowed her head. "*Grazie*, Your Highness."

"But you, Christina, will be a real princess. And that demands something special from a woman. The reward is something special in return." She picked up an ornate, medium-size box from the couch and slowly lifted the lid. A glimmering tiara rested on a bed of white velvet.

Christina put a hand to her throat. "Valentina."

"I wore this when I married Antonio's father. It must stay in my family, but you would honor me if you wore it when you marry my son."

Tears glistened in Christina's eyes. "It's beautiful." Diamonds and sapphires swirled together in gradually bigger scrolls until they overlapped in the front, creating a heart. "It's too much."

"Nonsense. A princess needs a tiara," Valentina insisted. "It would please me very much."

Christina sent Lindsay a pleading look. What should she do?

Lindsay gave a small shrug. "It's something borrowed and something blue."

"Oh, my." Christina gave a small laugh. "You said the items would come."

"I must go." Valentina handed the box to Christina. "Try it on with your dress and veil, you will see. A security officer will stay behind to collect it until the wedding."

"Valentina." Christina gripped the other woman's hand. *"Grazie."*

"Ciao, my dears." With a wave of her fingers, the queen breezed out the door.

Immediately the room felt as if a switch had been flipped and the energy turned off.

Giana Russo excused herself and followed behind Valentina.

Christina sighed, her gaze clinging to Zach. "And I'm supposed to follow that?"

Lindsay's gut tightened. She'd soothed many a nervous bride. But a nervous queen-to-be? That was out of her league. She sent Zach a pleading look.

He didn't hesitate. He went to Christina and wrapped her in a warm hug. "She's a force of nature, no denying that. Everyone likes Valentina. She's fun and vivacious." He stepped back at the perfect moment. "But what Halencia needs now is warm and constant. And that's you."

"*Grazie*, Zach." Christina's shoulders relaxed with his words. "I am glad you came today."

"Of course. Hey, listen. I'm sorry for sitting on your dress. I'll pay for all the repairs and alterations."

"You sat on my dress?" Christina's surprise showed on her face. "Lindsay said some beading came loose during the travel."

"With a little help from my butt." He glanced at Lindsay over his shoulder, gratitude warming his whiskey eyes. "She seems to think Signora Russo can do *magia* and fix it."

"*Si, si.* I can fix." Giana blew back into the room. An attendant followed behind and carried Christina's beautiful gown into one of the dressing rooms. "I have looked at the damage. It is not so bad. A little re-stitching will solve everything."

"Nonna!" A little girl ran into the room. Adorable, with big brown eyes and a cap of short, wild curls, she clutched a bright pink stuffed dog under arm. She came to a stop when she spotted three strangers with her grandmother.

"Ah, Lucette. *Scusa il bambina*." Giana tried to pick up the toddler but she squealed and ducked behind Christina. "My apologies. We had a small emergency and I was recruited to babysit. My daughter should be here shortly to get her. Lucette, come to Nonna."

"Oh, she's no trouble. *Ciao*, Lucette." Christina bent at the knees so she was on the same level as the little girl, who stared at her with big, beautiful eyes. "What's your doggy's name?"

Lucette giggled and held out the dog. She jabbered a mouthful of words that made no sense to Lindsay at all. She looked at Zach but he shook his head, indicating he didn't understand the words, either.

"What a lovely name." Christina apparently made the dog's name out or pretended to. She chatted with the child for another few minutes, making the girl laugh. From her ease with the little one, it was obvious Christina loved children. Her gentleness and genuine interest delighted Giana's granddaughter until a harried assistant hurried into the room and swept the girl up.

"Scusa." The young assistant bobbed her head and left with the little girl.

Giana sighed. "Such excitement today. Are you ready, Signorina Rose, to try on your dress?"

Christina nodded. She and Giana disappeared into one of the dressing rooms.

Lindsay and Zach looked at each other.

"Do we stay or go?" Zach asked.

"I'm going to stay until she comes out." Lindsay sat facing the occupied dressing room. "She may want company for the whole appointment. You can go if you want. I'm sure she'd understand."

"I'll wait to see how long you're going to be." He settled next to her. Way too close. His scent reached her, sensual and male, distracting her so she almost missed his question. "Have you ever come close to being the bride?"

"Not really." She smoothed the crease in her pale beige pants. "The one time I even contemplated it, I found out the relationship existed more in my imagination than in reality."

Interest sparked behind his intelligent gaze.

"How about you?" She tried to sidetrack him.

"Once," he admitted. "How do you get to marriage in your imagination? You're too levelheaded to make up what's not there."

"Thanks for that." She uncrossed and then recrossed her legs, creating distance between them on the couch though her new position had her facing him. "He was my high school sweetheart. We got split up during our senior year when his parents moved away."

"That's tough."

She chanced a quick peek at him through her lashes to see if he truly understood or was simply saying what he thought she wanted to hear. The intensity in his regard showed an avid interest, encouraging her to go on.

"It was tough. We just understood each other. I lost my best friend as well as my boyfriend." The crease on her right leg got the same smoothing action as her left. "I always felt he was the one who got away."

"But you reconnected."

"We did. When the royal wedding was announced last year, he saw a piece where it mentioned I was the event planner, so he looked me up in Hollywood."

"And you had fonder memories of him than he had for you?"

"You could say that." The gentle way he delivered the comment made it safe to look at him as she answered. "I was so surprised and happy to see him. My mom, too. She's always on me to find a man. At first it was as though Kevin and I'd never been apart." Because of their past connection, he'd skipped right under her shields. "We were having lots of fun just hanging out and catching up. But I was so busy. Especially after word I'd been chosen to handle Antonio's wedding started to get around.

"Kevin was a freelance writer, so his schedule was flexible and he offered to help. I didn't want to take advantage, but I wanted to be with him. I let him tend bar at a few of the smaller events. That went well, so he started pushing to work the weddings."

"This is where the but comes in?"

Lindsay nodded, went back to plucking at her crease.

Zach's hand settled over hers, stilling the nervous motion.

She calmed under his touch. Under the sympathy in his eyes.

It still hurt to recall what a fool she'd been.

"First I got a warning from one of my vendors. He didn't know we were involved and he said I should keep an eye on the new bartender. He'd seen him outside with one of the guests."

"Bastard."

"It gets worse. And it's my own fault."

"How is it your fault when he's the one cheating?"

Good question. Too bad she didn't have a good answer.

"Because I let him charm me. When I asked him about what the vendor had seen, he didn't get defensive or act guilty. He had a story ready that the woman told him she was feeling sick so he'd walked her outside, hoping fresh air would help. I had no reason not to believe him. It explained what the vendor saw and... Kevin could be very solicitous."

"But it happened again."

Her head bobbed; perfect representation for the bobble-head she'd been.

"He tried to explain that one away, too. But I was starting to wise up. I should have ended it then." But that ideal from the past lingered in her heart, overriding the urging of her head. "Before things started going south, I'd been invited to a big wedding of a studio head and asked Kevin to go with me. I didn't want to go alone and I wasn't working so I thought it would be okay." She blinked back tears. "I should have known what he wanted. The clues were there."

"He was using you."

"Oh, yeah. He always wanted to know who everyone was. I thought he was just starstruck by the movers and shakers of Hollywood. The truth was he had a script he was shopping. I found him messing around with a well-known producer."

"Male or female?"

That surprised a bark of laughter from her; the moment of levity easing her rising tension. "Female. But thanks for that perspective. I guess it could have been worse."

"Bad enough. He hurt you."

"Yes. But only because I saw what I wanted to see."

"The possibility of a wedding for the wedding planner?"

"How is it you can see me so clearly?" she demanded.

It was uncanny how he saw straight to her soul. She hadn't been half as sad at losing Kevin as she had been to lose a boyfriend with marriage potential. She wanted what she gave to all her clients. A lovely wedding, in a spectacular venue, with friends and family surrounding her as she pledged her love. She longed for it with all her heart.

Kevin had stolen that from her. He'd given her hope, dangled the reality within her reach, only to yank it away. He was a user with no real affection or respect for her.

He'd seduced her for her contacts. And, yeah, that hurt. Her pride had taken a huge hit and the experience had left her more relationship-shy than ever. But it had taken less than a week for her to recognize it was more work-related than personal. He could have damaged her reputation. She'd worked twice as hard since the breakup to make sure it didn't happen again.

And she shored up her defenses to keep from letting anyone close enough to use her again. Or hurt her.

"Because it's all right here." Zach responded to the question about seeing her so clearly by stroking his thumb over her cheek. "There's no deception in you, Lindsay. You're open and giving and articulate."

"You're saying I'm an open book. How flattering." Not.

"I'm saying there's no artifice in you. When you interact with someone, they know they're getting the real you—straightforward good or bad. Do you know what a gift that is? To know you can trust what's being presented to you without having to weigh it for possible loopholes and hidden agendas?"

"Politics," she said dismissively.

"School. Business. Friends. Dates." He ran down a list. Then, too restless to sit, he rose to pace. "For as far back as I can remember I've known not to take anything at face value. My nannies used to praise me for being a good kid then lie about my behavior to get a raise."

"That's terrible." What a sad lesson for a child to learn. "You said you almost got close to a wedding. What happened? Is it what put you off big, fancy weddings?"

"It never got that far." He fell silent and fingered a wisp of lace edging a floor-length veil. Then he moved to one glittering with diamonds and, finally, to one of lace and the opalescence of pearls.

As the silence lengthened, she knew an answer wasn't coming. And then he surprised her.

"Luckily I learned before it was too late that it wasn't me she wanted but the Sullivan name." The lack of emotion in his reply spoke volumes.

He didn't add more. He didn't have to. After a childhood of indifference, he'd fallen for a woman only to learn she had more interest in his family name than in the man who carried that name.

Lindsay felt his pain. Shockingly so. Meaning he was getting under her skin. That shouldn't be happening; her shields were firmly in place. Zach just refused to acknowledge them. And he was getting to her.

She wanted to know more, to ask what happened, but she'd been wrong to get so personal. They weren't on a date. They were working. She had no right to dig into his past when she insisted theirs was a professional relationship.

Yet she was disappointed. She rarely talked about herself, never exposed her heart like that. And he'd responded, obviously reluctant to share but reciprocating just the same. How unfair that life should send her this man when all her attention needed to be focused on her job.

He lifted the lace-and-pearl veil and carried it to her.

"What are you doing?" she breathed.

Pulling her to her feet, he turned her and carefully inserted the combs of the veil in her hair. The exquisite lace flowed around her, making her feel like a bride even in a sleeveless beige-linen pant suit.

"Imaging you as a bride." His breath whispered

over her temple. "What would you choose for yourself, Lindsay?"

"I'm like you," she said as he led her toward a three-way mirror. Why was she letting him do this? "I want small, intimate."

"But with all the trimmings?"

"Of course. Oh, my." The pearls on the lace gave it a glow. He'd placed the veil just under her upswept bun. The lace caressed her arms as it fell down her back in an elegant waterfall of tulle and lace and pearls. It had such presence it made her beige pantsuit appear bridal.

The picture in the mirror stole her breath. Made her longing for what eluded her come rushing back.

She'd hoped coming to Tuscany, managing the royal wedding, would help her get her wedding mojo back. Peering into the mirror she realized that would only happen when she opened herself to love again. Sweat broke out on her upper lip at the very notion of being that vulnerable.

"I love the pearls against your sunshine-brown hair." Zach brushed the veil behind her shoulder and met her gaze in the mirror. "You're going to make a beautiful bride."

With him standing beside her in his dress shirt and black pants the reflection came too close to that of a bride and groom. Her heels brought her up to his shoulder. They actually looked quite stunning together.

She swallowed hard and took a giant step backward, reaching up at the same time to remove the veil. She was in so much trouble.

"I'm the planner, not the bride," she declared. "I don't have time to play make-believe." Handing him the veil, she retreated to the couch and her purse. Time to put fanciful thoughts aside and call Christina's aunt to set up an appointment on their way home.

Because she'd liked the image in the mirror way too much for her peace of mind.

Just Lindsay's luck. Christina's aunt Pia couldn't meet with them until five in the evening. She ran through her current to-do list in her head, looking for something she could check off.

"Oh, no, you don't." Zach tugged on her ponytail. "You've worked nonstop this past week. We are due some rest and relaxation. We're in the lovely city of Milan. I say we play tourist."

Okay, there were worse ways to spend the afternoon than wandering the streets with a handsome man on her arm.

Lunch at an open café on the Naviglio Grande—a narrow canal with origins in the 1100s used to transport the heavy marble to the middle of the city where the Duomo di Milano was being built—was a true delight. As was strolling along the canal afterward and checking out the antique stores and open-air vendors.

A lovely candleholder at a glassblower's stall caught her eye. How perfect for the reception tables. They had a flat bottom and five-inch glass petals spiked all the way around to create a floral look. The piece had presence but was short enough to converse over without being in the way. And she loved that it came in so many colors. She wanted the one with spiking gold petals. It reminded her of sunflowers.

"I'd like to order two hundred, but I need them within two weeks. Can you do that?" The young artist's eyes popped wide.

"Si. Si," he eagerly assured her. "I have ready."

"Why so many?" Zach asked. "And don't you already have candleholders with the royal crest on them?"

"Yes, but I think the clear glass bowls etched with the royal crest will sit nicely right in the middle of these and be absolutely gorgeous with a candle inside. A win-win." She got a beautiful, unique presentation that was both fragile and bold, and the palace got their staid, boring candleholders used.

"That's pretty genius." He applauded her.

"It's my job to mix the styles and needs of the bride and groom into a beautiful event that's appealing to them individually and as a couple."

"I'm learning there's more to this wedding planning stuff than I ever would have believed."

"Yeah. I'll convert you yet."

"Now, that's just crazy talk."

She sent him a chiding glance. "I want two hundred because I want plenty for my reception tables, but I also think the candleholders will make good gifts for the guests. What do you think, best man? Christina has pretty much left the decisions up to me and you're Antonio's stand-in. Do you think this would make a good gift for the guests to take away?"

He blinked at her for a moment, clearly surprised to have his opinion sought. He rubbed his chin as he contemplated the candleholder she held. "It's a pretty sophisticated crowd, but, yeah. Each piece is unique. That will appeal to the guests while the piece will also act as a reminder of the event."

"Then it will have served its purpose."

She turned back to the vendor. "In two weeks," she repeated, needing to know his excitement wasn't overriding his capabilities.

"*Si, si...due* weeks. I work night and day."

Given he would be working with heat and glass, she wasn't sure that was a good idea. She made a note in her tablet to check on his progress in a week. If he wasn't going to make it, she'd adjust her order to cover the tables only. And just give the royal crest candleholders away as a gift. But she really hoped he could pull it off.

She gave him her card with her email, asked him to send her a purchase order and advised him he'd have to sign a confidentiality agreement. His hand shook as he took the card, but he nodded frantically and handed Zach the package containing the sample she'd bought.

Zach made the next purchase. A Ferrari California T convertible. She thought they were just window shopping when he dragged her to the dealership. There was no denying the cars were sexy beasts. And it seemed the height of luxury to have the showroom on the fifth floor.

Even when Zach started talking stats and amenities, she blew it off. Nobody walked into a Ferrari dealership and walked out with a car. Or they shouldn't. It was a serious investment and required serious thought.

But Zach stood, hands on hips, surveying the slick car and nodding his head to whatever the salesman was saying. The portly man spoke English with such a thick accent she didn't know how Zach understood him.

"What color?" Zach asked her.

Her turn to blink at him in surprise at having her opinion sought. "What?"

"What color do you like better? The red or the black?"

"Are you insane? You can't just walk in here and buy a car."

"I'm pretty sure I can."

"But—"

"I've been thinking of buying one," he confessed. "I'm stoked at the idea of buying it here in Italy, from the original dealership. And it'll be nice to have a car since the rental company hasn't replaced the Land Rover yet."

She eyed the beautiful, sleek cars. "They'll probably have it replaced before they can deliver one of these."

"Pixie, they could have a car ready in an hour. But they have one downstairs with all the amenities I want. I could drive it back to Monte Calanetti if I wanted."

"Oh, my dog. You're serious about this."

He grinned, flashing his dimple and looking younger and as satisfied as a teenaged boy getting his first car.

"It's the California T series. I have to have one, right? I deserve something for closing the government deal. What color?" he demanded again.

Okay, she got it. He sought a physical treat for recent accomplishments because he wasn't getting any emotional accolades. Who could blame him? Not her.

"Indeed you do." Adjusting her mood to his, she

glanced around the show room. "You don't want red or black. Too cliché."

"I'd use the word classic."

"I like that pretty blue. It reminds me of the sea around Halencia. If you're taking a souvenir home, it should represent where you've been."

"The blue." His inclined his head, his brown eyes reflecting his appreciation of her comeback. "Hmm." He strolled over to look it over better. "I'm not really looking for pretty."

"Is rockin' a better adjective? More masculine? We can use that if you prefer, because it's a rockin' pretty blue."

"I like rockin'."

"But do you like the blue?"

"I do. Though the classics are nice, too."

"They're cliché for a reason."

"Signora." The salesman flinched, unable to stay silent any longer. *"Per favore*, not say cliché."

"Scusa," she apologized, sending Zach an unrepentant smirk.

He said something in Italian to the salesman, who nodded and stepped away.

"I have to do this," he said, lifting her chin on his finger and lowering his mouth to cover hers as if he couldn't wait another moment to taste her.

CHAPTER NINE

THE FLAVOR OF him filled her senses. Oh. Just, oh.

She should protest, step away, remind him of their professional status. She did none of those things. Instead she melted against him, lifting her arms around his neck.

How she'd missed his touch. She thrilled at his hands on her waist pulling her closer, at his body pressed to hers from mouth to knees, the two of them fitting together like cogs and grooves. This was more dangerous than watching their reflection in the mirror at Signora Russo's. By far.

Didn't matter. She sank into sensation as she opened to him. More than she should in a Ferrari dealership. Or maybe not. They were hot cars, after all.

A throat clearing loudly announced the return of the salesman.

Zach lifted his head, nipped her lower lip.

"Hold on." She ducked her head against him, turning away from the salesman.

"What are you doing?" He spoke gently and cradled her head. Perfect.

"Saving you some money. Tell our friend over there that you're sorry, but I'm totally embarrassed and want to leave."

He rattled off a few words of Italian. Predictably the salesman protested.

She pushed at Zach, making a show of wanting to leave. "Tell him you'll have to buy the car when you get back to the States because we're leaving Milan tonight and probably won't make it back here."

While he conveyed her message, she grabbed his hand and began pulling him toward the exit, carefully avoiding the salesman's gaze.

The salesman responded in a conciliatory tone, his voice growing closer as he spoke.

"He just dropped the price by ten thousand dollars," Zach advised her.

She frantically shook her head and, holding his hand in both of hers, she bracketed his arm and buried her face in his shoulder. "Let's see if we can get him to twenty. Shake your head sadly, put your arm around me and head for the elevator."

"You know I can afford the car."

"So not the point."

"What was the point again?"

"Trust me. He's not going to let you walk away."

He sighed, then she felt the movement of his head

and his arm came around her. She leaned into him as they walked toward the elevator.

"I can't believe I'm leaving here without a car."

"You can always order it online and have them deliver it. If he lets you walk away."

"You owe me dinner for this."

They got all the way to the elevator before the salesman hailed Zach. He rushed over, all jovial and solicitous, giving his spiel as he approached. The elevator doors opened just as he arrived next to them. The man opened his arms wide in a gesture that welcomed Zach to consider what a good deal was being offered.

Zach nodded. *"Si, avete un affare."*

"You took the offer?"

"I have. And you're invited to visit the gift shop and pick out a gift while I finalize things here."

"Oh. Nice touch. Okay, you can buy the car." She stepped into the elevator. "Don't be long."

Thirty minutes later he collected her from the gift shop and they headed out. On the street he pulled her into his arms and gave her a long, hard kiss. Then he draped his arm around her shoulders and started walking.

"That's the most fun I've had in a long time."

"How much?"

"For twenty-five thousand less than quoted."

"Aha! So you owe me dinner."

"You have skills, Pixie."

"I have a few tricks. I'm always working with a budget whether it's five hundred dollars or five million, so I've learned to negotiate for my job. I enjoy the challenge. You have money. You're used to buying what you want without worrying about the cost."

"I've negotiated for my business."

"But that's different, isn't it? You're on the sales side then, demanding value for services. When it comes to buying—"

"I want the best regardless of price. It's how I was raised."

"You were fortunate." As soon as the words left her mouth she remembered what he'd said about people in his life always having an agenda even when he was a young child and how his parents brushed aside his success to make demands of him. Money didn't make up for everything. She quickly changed the subject.

"So, are you driving home? Am I visiting Christina's aunt on my own?"

"I'm going with you. I went with the blue car, which needed modified for some of the upgrades I wanted. They'll be delivering the car in a couple of days. We have an hour before we need to meet the helicopter. Do you want to go see the cathedral?"

He was right. Today had been fun. She couldn't remember when she'd last let go and played for a day. She liked playing tourist. Wanted it to continue.

She sighed, knowing she needed to rein them in.

A bell kept pinging in her brain, warning her to stop the foolishness, reminding her of the danger of surrendering to his charm. Hadn't she already rehashed all this with herself at the fitting?

Yes, and she knew what she risked if she continued to let her emotions rule her actions.

Yet she still reached up and tangled her fingers with his at her shoulder.

"It'll be rushed, but it sounds like fun."

"Okay, let's go." He stepped to the curb and waved down a taxi. "At least we'll get to see it. And if we really want to see more, we can plan a day when we can come back and do a full tour."

Her heart soared at the way he linked them into the future.

She deserved this time. Work always came first and because the nature of it was so party central she experienced a faux sense of having an active social life. For too long she'd suppressed her loneliness. Just this once she'd let loose and enjoy the history and charm of an ancient city in the company of a gorgeous man totally focused on her.

Sliding into the back of the cab, she smiled when Zach linked their hands. And sighed when he leaned in for a kiss.

Tomorrow could take care of itself.

Zach in a Speedo was a piece of art.

He swam once or twice a day. She remembered

from her research that he'd met Antonio on the Harvard swim team. Obviously he still enjoyed the water. And she enjoyed him.

Funny how his swims always seemed to coincide with her need for a break. Uh-huh, a girl was allowed her illusions.

And she could look as long as she didn't touch.

The man was grace in motion. Watching that long, tanned, toned body move through the water gave her a jolt that rivaled caffeine. It was one fine view in a villa full of spectacular views and it made Lindsay's mouth water with want.

Now that she knew how it felt to brush up against that fine body, she longed for more. But she was back in the real world so she turned away from the sight of Zach striding confident and wet from the pool.

She took a sip from her soda, needing the wet and the cool. And drained it before she was through. Leaving the empty can on the bar she joined her assistant at the lovely oak table Zach had purchased for her use.

She pulled up her email and sent Christina a message to let her know they were still on the hunt for the brooch. As Christina had warned her Aunt Pia had been leery about talking to them, but with Christina's note she'd finally softened. She'd given the brooch to her daughter, but the younger woman hadn't worn it for her wedding, either. Pia had called her daughter while they were there and she couldn't recall what had happened to the brooch. Pia suggested Sophia might know.

Lindsay would be meeting with Sophia tomorrow, two weeks from the wedding.

"Serena, can you call and remind Louisa that Zach and I will be meeting the landscapers at the palazzo this morning."

The two of them were set to leave in a few minutes and she needed work to help her get the visual of his nearly nude body out of her head.

"Already done. And I sent the information to the glassblower as you requested. He already confirmed delivery for a week before the wedding."

"Excellent."

Serena turned out to be a godsend. She looked cool and competent in blue jeans and a crisp white tee, her long black hair slicked back in a ponytail that nearly reached her waist. And she was every bit as efficient as she appeared.

"Let's put it on the calendar to check with him in a few days to be sure he's on schedule. If I have to find another gift, I'd rather know sooner than later."

"*Si*, I put a note on your calendar."

"Perfect."

They went over a few other items, scratching off two on the to-do list and adding three. "The palace rep is supposed to take care of ordering the table and chairs, but can you call to make sure they have and confirm what they've ordered."

Her brown eyes rounded. "You want me to check the palace's work?"

"Yes. There's no room for misunderstandings. I need to know every detail is covered."

The girl nodded. "*Si*, I will call them."

"Good. I know this may be a hard concept for you, Serena, but until this wedding is over, your first loyalty is to me. It's my job to give the prince and Christina a beautiful wedding that will represent the house of L'Accardi well. You have no idea how many errors I've found by following up on details handled by other people. Some have been innocent mistakes, but others were outright sabotage."

"That's terrible!"

Lindsay nodded. "If I hadn't caught the mistakes, intentional or otherwise, not only would the bride and groom have been disappointed and possibly embarrassed, but my reputation would have suffered badly."

"*Si*. I will check every detail."

"*Grazie*. And don't forget to find a nice, understated dress for the occasion. Something in light blue."

Serena's brown eyes rounded even bigger than before. "I am to attend the royal wedding?" It was a near squeak.

"You'll be working it with me, yes."

"Oh, my goodness! I have to shop!"

Lindsay smiled. "After you check on the table and chairs."

"Si." Serena nodded, her eagerness offset by a desperate look in her eyes.

"And bring me the receipt. It's a work expense."

Relief flooded the girl's features. *"Grazie."*

"Are you ready to go?" A deep male voice filled the room.

Zach stood in the doorway to the house, thankfully fully dressed in jeans and a brown T-shirt that matched his eyes.

"Ready." Lindsay grabbed her purse and dropped her tablet inside. "Let's go."

The wind whipped through her hair as Zach drove them across town in the golf cart. He pulled straight into the drive.

Two things struck her right away. Louisa was in the middle of a heated discussion on her doorstep. Her opponent towered over her smaller frame. He had dark hair, broad shoulders and a wicked-fine profile.

And second, construction paraphernalia had been cleared away but the grounds were only a quarter cleared.

"What the heck, Zach?" Lindsay demanded as she climbed out of the golf cart. "I thought you hired someone to clean this all out."

"I did and I take full responsibility for the mess-up. I hired the crew the mayor recommended and I told them to clear out all the weeds but to save the original plants."

"No, no, no. Everything was supposed to be cleared out."

He grimaced. "I'm hearing that now, at the time I was answering a text from my office. I got it wrong. I'm sorry."

"They didn't even do what you asked." She stomped forward, scanning the dry brush and overgrown ground cover. "The landscaping team is going to be here any minute. The construction team is scheduled to start the day after they're done. This needed to be done already."

This couldn't be happening. She'd had everything planned down to the last minute. There were acres to clear. The whole property needed to be in shape, not just the area around the chapel and palazzo.

"Lindsay, I'm sorry."

Lindsay swung around to Louisa. The other woman stood huddled into herself, the tall man she'd been arguing with at her side.

"This is my fault," Louisa said. "I've been distracted the past few days. I should have noticed the grounds weren't being cleared out like they should be."

"No. It's mine. I should have been checking on the progress." Follow up on every detail. Hadn't she just pressed that fact home with Serena? She'd been the one to drop the ball.

"Placing blame does no good." Zach refused to play the role of dunce. He'd made this mess. It was up to him to clean it up. "We need to focus on a solution."

"He's right." Hands on his hips, the tall man Louisa had been arguing with surveyed the grounds. "You must be Lindsay Reeves, the wedding planner. Nico Amatucci." He held out his hand as he introduced himself. "I own the vineyard next door."

"Right." She shook his hand, appreciated the firm grip. "We're serving your wine at the reception. I've sampled some. It's very good."

"Zach Sullivan, best man." Zach inserted his hand between the two of them, not caring for the admiration in Amatucci's gaze as it ran over Lindsay. Some distance between the two suited Zach fine.

No way was Zach letting the other man play hero while he chafed under the restraint of his plan. It didn't help that his gut roiled with guilt at seeing Lindsay so upset.

He was making her work harder than she needed to on the most important event of her career. Watching her blame herself for something he'd done didn't sit well, no matter how well-intentioned his plan had been.

Especially when he had nothing to show for it.

Neither Tony nor Christina showed any signs of

backing out of the wedding. The two of them had managed to distance themselves from what went on in Monte Calanetti so any delays Lindsay suffered were mere blips on their radars.

Zach had only managed one meeting with Tony, but whenever he broached the topic on their hurried calls, Tony shut him down. Christina did the same when Zach got a few minutes alone with her at the fitting, though he had to give her points for being much more polite about it.

"I'm not sure how this happened." Zach gritted his teeth as he played his part for his audience of three. "I was telling Lindsay I hired the crew Mayor Alonso recommended. He mentioned the owner had just broken up with his girl, but I didn't figure that signified."

"Are you talking about Fabio?" Nico ran his hand through his dark hair. "He gets *molto* messed up when he and Terre are fighting, and he is no good for anything."

"I need to call him, get him out here." Lindsay took out her tablet. "This needs to be finished today. If he can't get it done, I need to get someone who can."

"Let me talk to him, *signorina*," Nico offered, his tone grim. "His girl is *incinta*. Fabio needs the work. I will make sure it gets done."

Lindsay hesitated then slowly nodded.

Seeing the despair in her indomitable blue eyes

shredded Zach. He decided right then to stop messing with her. Why should she suffer for Tony and Christine's stubbornness?

She shouldn't.

No more than he should be forced to play the fool.

The trip to Milan rated as one of the best days of his life. He'd enjoyed spending time with Lindsay, more than anyone he could remember in a long time. She was smart and fun, and too restrained, which challenged him to loosen her up. And she constantly surprised him. He marveled at her performance at the Ferrari dealership.

Her ex had given her enough grief. Zach wouldn't add to it.

He'd still try talking sense into the couple. For all the good it would do him. But no more messing with the wedding.

"Fabio's going to need help getting this all done," Zach announced, feeling the need to fix the problem. "Who else can we get to help?"

"I can call my men over to lend a hand for a few hours," Nico offered.

"Thanks, that's a start. I'm going to call the mayor."

"I'll help," Louisa stated. "It'll feel good to get outside and do some physical labor for a change."

Zach lifted his brow at that. The temperature topped eighty and the palazzo was in a valley. There was little in the way of a breeze to offset the mugginess from the clouds overhead.

"It is too hot for you," Nico told her bluntly. "You will stay inside."

Wrong move, buddy. Zach watched the storm brew in the palazzo owner's light blue eyes. She was almost guaranteed to work harder and longer than she would have if the other man had kept his mouth shut. But her offer gave him an idea.

"No," Louisa informed Nico, her chin notched up, "I will not. I'm partially responsible for this situation and I want to help."

"Me, too," Lindsay piped in. "Louisa, do you have an extra pair of gloves? We can get started while Nico contacts Fabio."

"I do. I have a scarf, too. You'll want to put your hair up."

The women wandered off. Nico glared after them. "She never listens."

Zach cleared his throat and clapped Nico on the shoulder. "My man, let me give you some advice. Rather than order a woman about, it's better to make her think it's her idea to start with."

Nico grimaced. "I know this. But she drives me… *pazzo.*"

"Crazy? I know the feeling. Perhaps when she starts to weary you can casually mention how thirsty the workers look and she'll go inside to provide refreshments."

"You misunderstand. There is nothing between

us," Nico clarified with more emphasis than necessary. "As there is between you and Ms. Reeves."

"If you asked her, she would say there is nothing between us, either."

Nico scowled.

Zach laughed. "You should call me Zach, as we'll be working together." And they got to work.

The whole town came out to help. Or so it seemed. The mayor arrived shortly after a remorseful Fabio. Alonso didn't ask what needed to be done. He wore khaki pants and an old denim shirt with the sleeves rolled up to his elbows. He picked up a shovel and got to work.

Lindsay called Serena and she showed up with a few friends, four of Nico's men arrived in a pickup, including his brother Angelo. Eva's son, Mario, and a pack of early teens pitched in. The barber closed his shop to help. And on and on it went. Even the landscaping crew joined in, helping to haul debris and refuse away.

Everyone was happy and laughing.

At some point Lindsay was introduced to Vincenzo Alberti, the director of tourism. When she expressed her gratitude, he explained that the whole town was proud the royal wedding was happening there. That they wanted their city to be represented well and that they were all excited to be a part of it in some way.

Lindsay wiped at the sweat on forehead with a towel she'd tucked into her waistband and surveyed their progress. Another hour should see it done. A good thing as it would be dark not long after.

She was hot and sticky, tired and sore. And hungry.

She imagined everyone else was, too. But no one was leaving. They all meant to see it finished. Nico and Louisa had put their animosity aside to coordinate the workers' efforts.

"Almost done." Zach appeared beside her, his tanned and muscular chest on full display. As had many of the men, he'd ditched his shirt somewhere along the way.

She resisted the urge to run her palm down his sweaty abs. More than once she'd caught herself admiring the flex and flow of muscle and tendon under smooth flesh. Dark and tanned, he fit right in with the Halencians. Fit and toned, he matched the laborers pace for pace.

He was poetry in motion and she had a hard time keeping her attention fixed on her chore. Especially with him standing in front of her.

"I'm amazed by the support we got from everyone." Rather than look at him she watched the landscapers fill their truck with bags of weeds. "I wish there was something we could do for them."

"I was thinking the same thing." He took her towel and wiped the back of her neck, sending tingles down her spine where his fingers trailed over her skin. "I thought about hosting a party at the villa, but I prefer to reward everyone now, so I asked Alonso for a suggestion. He mentioned Mancini's. I called and talked to the owner. Raffaele Mancini said he'd open up the patio for us and put a nice meal together."

"'Nice' is the operative word there, champ. Mancini's is catering the wedding. Eva also told me about Mancini's as an option for an upscale meal. I'm not sure I can afford that."

"I'm covering it."

"You don't have to do that."

"I insist. I feel this is mostly my fault. Paying for dinner is a small enough thing to do. Plus, Mancini heard about what happened and apologized for not making it over here to help out. So he's giving us a discount."

The spirit of this town just kept amazing her.

"Shall we start passing the word? Mancini's at eight. That'll give Raffaele time to cook. And the rest of us time to clean up."

Dinner turned into a party. When Lindsay stepped inside, assisted by Zach's hand at the small of her back, she got pulled into a big hug by the maître d', who was a curvy blonde with bright gray eyes and a smile so big she beamed.

"Hello. Welcome to Mancini's." Surprisingly the

bubbly blonde was American. Then she announced why she was so excited, "Winner of the Italian Good Food Award!"

"Wow." Lindsay knew the award was on par with the Michelin Star in France. "Congratulations. That's fantastic."

Zach echoed her. "Raffaele didn't mention it when I spoke to him earlier."

"We just heard an hour ago. You must be Lindsay Reeves and Zach Sullivan, the wedding planner and best man. I'm Daniella, Rafe's fiancée. We have the patio all set up for you. Some people have already started to arrive. You'll have to excuse us if we're a little giddy tonight. We're over the top about the award."

"As you should be," Zach said easily. "I hope you, Raffaele and the staff can join us later for a congratulatory toast."

That smile flashed again. "I'm sure that can be arranged. I'll tell Rafe."

The patio was enclosed but the large windows were wide open, letting in the cool evening air. Wine bottles hung from the overhead beams along with green ivy. Red-checked tablecloths covered two large picnic tables that seated twenty each and three round tables at the far end.

A couple of extra chairs were needed, but everyone shuffled around so everyone got seated. Alonso arranged it so he and Vincenzo sat with Lindsay and Zach along with Nico and Louisa.

Raffaele had "thrown together" a steak Florentine for them that melted in Lindsay's mouth. She was definitely putting it on the wedding menu.

She wondered if Raffaele knew how to make *cornettos*.

"I'm exhausted," Louisa told Lindsay toward the end of the delicious meal when they had the table to themselves. "But it's a good tired."

"It's the same for me." Lindsay sipped her wine. "We accomplished a lot today. The landscapers will start tomorrow and the owner assured me they would make up the lost time."

"That's great. I'm glad we were able to get it done for you."

"I'm so impressed with the townspeople. How they rallied together to help out and were so cheerful even working in the heat and mugginess."

"Well, they're all enjoying dinner. This was a nice gesture."

"Zach's the one to thank. But we were happy to do it. Everyone worked so hard. I can tell you I've decided to order some big fans for the wedding and reception. I want the guests to be comfortable."

Louisa clinked her wineglass against Lindsay's. "I like the way you think. I'm sorry I dropped the ball."

"Don't sweat it. You worked as hard as anyone today." Lindsay eyed Zach talking with Nico, Alonso and a couple of other men near the bar. "And I know how easy it is to get distracted."

"Are the two of you involved?" Louisa asked.

Lindsay's gaze whipped back to her fellow American.

"There's a...tension between the two of you," the woman explained.

"He'd like there to be." Lindsay rolled the stem of her wineglass between her fingers, watched the liquid swirl as her thoughts ran over the past two weeks. "But I need to stay focused on the job. As today clearly proved."

"He can't take his eyes off you."

"And Nico keeps you in his sights. Is there something between the two of you? You seemed to be arguing this morning."

"We're always arguing." Louisa's gaze flicked over the man in question. Her expression remained as composed as always, but there was no hiding the yearning in her pale eyes. "That is why it's good there's nothing between us."

A loud cheer went through the patio. Lindsay glanced around to see Rafe and Danielle had joined the party. Another round of cheers sounded as waiters flowed through the room with trays of champagne glasses.

Alonso grabbed a flute and held it high. "*Primo*, a huge *grazie* to Raffaele and Mancini's for hosting us tonight on such short notice. And for the wonderful meal he provided." More cheers. "*Secondo*, we are all excited to be here to share in the joyous news of Mancini's receiving the Good Food Award!" He held his glass high. "We had no doubts, *amico mio*, none at all. *Complimenti!*"

"*Complimenti!*" The crowd clapped and cheered, lifting their glasses and sipping.

Rafe stood on a chair. "*Grazie, grazie.* I am happy so many of my friends could be here to share this with me tonight. Business picked up when Mancini's was chosen to feed the royal wedding guests. Now, we have the Good Food Award the tourists will come even more. Monte Calanetti is on the map!"

A roar of approval rose to the roof.

"Nice touch, sharing his success with the citizens." Zach slid into his seat. "Classy."

"Raffaele is good people," Louisa affirmed. "I'm going to congratulate him on my way out. Good night. Zach, thank you for dinner."

"My pleasure."

Louisa walked away, leaving Lindsay and Zach alone together. He picked up her hand. "You look tired."

"I am." Too tired to fight over possession of her hand. She really needed to tell him the day in Milan had been a mistake and they needed to regroup to where they'd been before the trip. But every touch weakened her resolve.

"I'm sorry I messed up." There was a quality to his voice she couldn't quite pinpoint. She dismissed it as fatigue and the fact he probably didn't have to apologize for his work effort very often. Like never.

"You thought you were hiring the best crew," she reminded him. "And, you know, I really enjoyed today, getting to know more of the local people, seeing how they all rallied around each other to help. It was an inspiring experience. As you said before, too often people are all about their own agendas. Today reinforced my view of humanity."

"Sometimes those agendas can be well-meaning." Again his tone was off.

"You mean like Fabio obsessing over his girl and their baby? I get that, but look at how many lives he impacted by not honoring his contract. Yes, I enjoyed the day, but the landscaper is still going to have to make up lost time, and I lost a whole day. Life is so much easier when people are up front with each other."

He brought her hand to his mouth and kissed her knuckles. "Let's go home and soak our aches away in the Jacuzzi."

Oh, goodness, that sounded wonderful.

And dangerous.

She'd promised herself she'd get her head on straight today, put her infatuation aside and focus on the job. It was the smart thing to do. All he wanted was a summer fling. She had only to recall how he'd clammed up after she'd shared her humiliating history with Kevin to realize his interest was strictly physical.

And still she tangled her fingers with his. "Let's go."

CHAPTER TEN

AFTER THE INTENSE heat of the day, the balmy softness of the night air caressed Lindsay's shoulders with the perfect touch of cool. The rest of her, submerged in the hot, roiling water of the spa, thanked her for her foolish decision.

"I really did need this." She rolled her neck, stretching the tendons.

Strong hands turned her and began to work at the tightness in her shoulders. "So much stress."

The low timbre of Zach's voice made her whole body clench in need. She tried to shift away, but he easily held her in place.

"I never would have thought a wedding would be so much work."

She bit her bottom lip to suppress a moan, not wanting to encourage him. "Why, because it's just a big party? It's more than that, you know. It's two people creating a life together. That requires the meshing of many moving parts. The bride and groom, family members, attendants and, in this case, palace representatives and dignitaries. And that's just on the day. Before that there's flowers, food, wine, cake, photographers, seating in the chapel, setting up for the reception. Seating arrangements. Thank you, once again, for your help with that. I got the final approval from the palace today."

"My pleasure."

There was that tone again. She glanced at him over her shoulder. "You stopped listening after family members, didn't you?"

"You caught me." He let her float away a bit before turning her so she faced him.

"What's up with you?" She brushed the damp hair off his furrowed brow. "You've been slightly off all night."

"Today was my fault."

So that was it. Zach was so laid-back with her she sometimes forgot he ran a multibillion-dollar company. He was used to being in control and being right.

"We already talked about this. Stop feeling guilty."

"You know how I feel about large weddings."

"So what? You deliberately hired someone you knew couldn't do the job? You're just feeling bad because you're a problem solver and today it took a lot of people to fix the problem. It's okay. You repaid them all with a very nice dinner. And they all got to celebrate Mancini's award with Raffaele. I didn't hear a single gripe from anyone today, so cut yourself some slack."

"It's not that. I can't help but think Tony and Christina are making a mistake."

"So you subconsciously sabotaged the cleanup?"

He looked away, staring out at the lights of Monte Calanetti. "Something like that. They barely know each other."

"They've been engaged for four years."

"And he's lived in America the whole time."

This was really tearing him up. So often since they'd met he'd been there for her when she'd needed him. She wished she had the magic words that would ease his concerns.

"They have no business getting married."

"Zach—" she rubbed his arm, hoping to soothe "—that's not for you to say."

"They're going to end up hating each other." The vehemence in his voice reinforced his distress. "I watched it happen to my parents. I can't stand to watch it happen to a man I think of as my brother."

She cupped his cheek, made him look at her. "No matter how much we love someone, we can't make their decisions for them. We wouldn't welcome them doing so for us and we owe them the same respect."

He sighed then pulled her into his lap, nuzzling the hair behind her ear. She wrapped her arms around him and hugged him tight. His arms enfolded her and they sat there for a while just enjoying the closeness of each other.

"She threw me over for my father."

Lindsay went still. "Who?"

"The woman I once got close to marrying."

"Oh, Zach." She tightened her grip on him and turning her head slightly, kissing him on the hard pec she rested against. "I'm so sorry."

"We met in college. My name didn't intimidate her, which was a real turn-on. It seemed all the girls I met were supplicants or too afraid to talk to me. Julia was a political science major. She said that was to appease her parents, that her real love was her minor, which were arts and humanities."

"She targeted you."

"Oh, yeah, she played me. Right from the beginning." He suddenly rose with her in his arms. "It's time to get out."

"I suppose we should." Her arms ringed his neck as he climbed out. She longed to hear more but had the sense if she pushed, he'd close down on her. So she kept it lighthearted. "I'm starting to prune."

He claimed her lips in a desperate kiss, holding her high against him as he devoured her mouth. His passion seduced her body just as his vulnerability touched her heart.

He carried her to the cabana where they'd left their towels. He released her legs and let her slide down his body. In her bare feet he towered over her, a dark shadow silhouetted by the nearly full moon. It took him a mere second to bridge the distance before his mouth was on hers again, hot and unsettling.

The right touch and she'd be lost to reason. From the reaction of his body to hers she knew he felt the same.

But he'd started his story and if she let this moment slip away, she may never hear the full tale.

She pulled back, leaning her brow on his damp chest while she caught her breath. "Tell me."

His hands tightened on her and then his chest lifted in a deep breath. He reached for her towel and wrapped it around her before grabbing his own.

She slid onto the double lounge and patted the cushion beside her. He joined her and pulled her into his arms so her back was to his front and the vista of Monte Calanetti spread out before them.

"She showed disinterest to catch my attention. And when I finally got her to go out with me, we just clicked so smoothly. We enjoyed all the same things. Had some of the same friends. She made me feel like she saw me, Zach Sullivan, as more than the son of William Sullivan. I reached the point where I was contemplating marriage. So I took her home to meet the parents. She was so excited. For the first time she asked me why I wasn't studying political science."

"With your family background, you'd think she'd ask that fairly early in the relationship."

"Yes, you'd think. I explained that I wanted nothing to do with politics. That technology was my passion. And I told her what she could expect with my parents. How they married to connect two politically powerful families and how they spent more time with others than with each other."

"And she went after your father."

"She barely spoke to me for the rest of the flight. I thought she was mulling it over, feared I'd put her off."

"You just gave her a new target." She held him tighter.

"She assumed because I grew up surrounded by politics that I didn't need to study it. And when I let her know I had no interest in it, and revealed my father liked to play discreetly, she went for the big guns. I caught them kissing in his study."

"I'm so sorry. I know how debilitating it is to walk in on a scene like that. The shock, the embarrassment, the betrayal. But I can't imagine how much worse it must hurt for her to be with your father."

With a double betrayal of this magnitude in his past, she kind of got why he didn't like big weddings. And why he was concerned for his friend.

"I just wanted out of there. My dad stopped me and said she'd be the one leaving. She'd come on to him, surprised him with the kiss. He wasn't interested. After she stormed off, he told me he may not be the best husband, but he'd never put a woman before his son."

"Well, that was good, to know he didn't betray you. Still, it's not something you can unsee."

He rested his head against hers, letting her know he sympathized with her, too. "It meant a lot. It's the single incident in my life I can look back on and know he put me first."

Wow, how sad was that? And yet when she looked at her own life, she couldn't find one instance that stood out like that. The difference was that her mom may put herself first, but Lindsay knew her mother loved her. From what Zach described, his folks rarely displayed affection.

She rolled her head against his chest, letting him know she understood his pain.

"So you've never gotten close to marriage since?"

"No. I've never met a woman I could see myself with five years from now let alone fifty. I don't ever want to end up like my folks. I want someone who will knock me off my feet."

"Good for you. That's what you should want. Hearing you say that about five years down the line, I realize I didn't have that with Kevin, either. I could see myself in a nice house with a couple of kids, but Kevin wasn't in the picture."

"I can see you in my future."

Her heart raced at his words and she had to swallow twice before she could answer. "Do you now?"

"Yes, all the way to tomorrow. I got a call from the dealership. The Ferrari will be here by nine. I thought we could drive to Sophia's."

She bit her lip, waffling a tad because she'd lost so much time today it was hard to justify the drive when the helicopter did the job so fast. Still she didn't want to make him feel even guiltier about today's events.

And, truly, how often did she get the chance to drive through the Halencia countryside in a Ferrari convertible with a handsome billionaire by her side?

This was probably a once-in-a-lifetime adventure. So why not stop fighting the inevitable and let the billionaire seduce her? She only had him for another couple of weeks. Less, really. She didn't want to look back and regret not knowing him fully.

Because she was very much afraid she'd be looking back a lot.

"Do I get to drive?"

"A little pixie like you? I don't think so." He laughed, his body shaking with the sound. The good cheer was wonderful to hear after his earlier despair.

"Come on. We both know it's not the size that matters, but what you do with it." His laughter shook her some more. "I feel I earned the opportunity to drive it at least once."

"We'll see."

"Oh, I'm driving." She snuggled into him. "I can tell it's going to be a lucky day."

"Yeah? How?"

"Well, if you're going to get lucky tonight, it seems only fair I get lucky tomorrow."

He picked her up as if she was no bigger than the pixie he called her and set her in his lap. Using the edge of his hand he tipped her face up to his and kissed her softly.

"Am I getting lucky? What about your strict policies?"

She brushed his hair back, enjoying the feel of the silky strands running through her fingers. "I should stay strong, but you are just too tempting, Mr. Sullivan."

He leaned forward and nipped her bottom lip. "I like the sound of that, Ms. Reeves. Shall we start with a bath in the claw-foot tub?"

How did he know she'd been dying to soak in that tub? It was a modern version of the old classic and could easily hold the two of them. She'd just been waiting for him to be gone long enough to slip into the master bathroom.

Something was still off with him. Why else suggest walking back to the house and risk her coming to her senses? Seated as she was in his lap, there was no doubting his desire for her. Maybe his attempts at humor hadn't quite rid him of his funk in talking about his near miss with wedded bliss.

Unwilling to risk him coming to his senses, she leaned into him, looped her arms around his neck and pressed her lips to his. "Why don't we start here?"

He needed no other prompting. He rolled her so she lay under him. Her head was cradled in one big hand holding her in place for his kiss that belied the fierceness of his embrace by being tender. He cherished her with his mouth; seducing her with soft thrusts and gentle licks until she melted in his arms.

He pulled back, his face unreadable in the darkness of the cabana. A finger traced slowly down the line of her jaw.

"I don't want to hurt you," he said, his breath warm against her skin.

"Then don't," she responded and pulled him back to her.

There were no more words after that, her mind too absorbed with sensation to put coherent thoughts together. The balmy night and towels served to dry them for the most part but she found a few stray drops of water on his side and he shivered when she traced her fingers through the drops, trailing the wet across his smooth skin.

It thrilled her to know her touch affected him as strongly as his did her. He stirred her with his gentleness, but he ignited her when his mouth became more insistent, his touch more demanding. She arched into him, seeking all he had to give.

He grinned against her mouth, assuring her he'd take care of her. A moment later her bikini top slipped away and he lavished attention on the exposed flesh. Her nipple puckered from the rush of heat on damp skin. And the agile use of his tongue.

Wanting nothing between them, she wiggled out of the rest of her suit and pushed at his. Despite her efforts, the damp cloth clung to him.

"Off." She panted against his mouth.

He pushed it down and off without leaving her side. She admired his efficiency almost as much as she admired his form. He was so beautiful she would have liked to see him but he felt too good in her arms for her to regret anything.

Especially when his mouth and fingers did such wicked things to her.

She felt more alive, more energized, more female than any other time in her life.

Being outside made it a hedonistic experience. The night breeze caressed heated skin, while the scent of roses perfumed the air. The rush of emotion compelled her to reach for the moon that hung so heavy in the sky.

Her senses reeled from an overload of sensation. He made her want, made her sizzle, made her mind spin.

When he joined them with an urgency that revealed he was as engaged as she was, she was excited to know she moved him, too. It made her bolder, braver, more determined to drive him insane with pleasure. She loved when he hissed through his teeth, when he kissed her as if he'd never get enough.

When he lost control.

When the connection they shared took her to a whole new level.

Never had she felt so close to another person, in body, in spirit, in heart. He lifted her higher, higher until together they soared through the stars and she shattered in the glow of the moon.

And later, after they roused and he led her to the house for a warm soak in the claw-foot tub and then landed in the comfort of his bed for a repeat performance, she knew for her this was more than two bodies seeking each other in the night.

Somewhere along the way, she'd fallen in love with the best man.

Lindsay stared out the window of the passenger seat in the Ferrari, brooding to the point where the beautiful countryside flew by unnoticed.

She'd had such a lovely morning with Zach. Waking snuggled in his arms, she'd waited for the regret to hit. But no remorse surfaced. She loved Zach. Being in his arms is where she wanted to be.

That would change when she had to walk away. In the meantime she'd make the most of every moment with him.

Watching him put the new Ferrari through its paces on the trip to Aunt Sophia's pleased her on a visceral level. Seeing his joy, absorbing his laughter, listening to him explain what made his new toy so special. His happiness made her happy, too.

The return trip was much more subdued, with Zach as quiet as she was.

Christina's aunt Sophia was a lovely woman, but a bit unorganized. Pia had called her, so she knew why they were there. She was so happy Christina wanted to wear the pin. Sophia had worn the brooch and she and her husband were still happily married after thirty-nine years.

Lindsay got her hopes up because Sophia seemed certain she had the brooch somewhere, but she'd already looked through her personal jewelry so she thought she must have stored it in the attic with other family heirlooms. Bad knees kept her from doing the search herself so she'd invited Lindsay and Zach to look all they'd like.

Luckily the attic was clean. And airy, once Zach opened the windows. But there was a lot to look through. She found a standing jewelry hutch and thought for sure the brooch would be there. Unfortunately not. Nor was it in any of the boxes or trunks they'd searched. In the end they'd left empty-handed.

"You okay?" Zach reached over and claimed her

hand. "You did everything you could to find the brooch."

"I know." She summoned a wan smile, grateful for his support. "I just hate to disappoint the bride. Especially Christina. I've never had a bride disassociate herself so completely from the process so close to the wedding. It's almost as if she's afraid to invest too much of herself into the wedding."

"She's dealing with a lot."

"I get that. That is why I really wanted to find the brooch." With a sigh she turned back to the window. "It's the one thing she seemed to latch onto. It kills me not to be able to find it for her."

The car slowed and then he pulled to the side of the road. She looked at him. "What's wrong? Is it something to do with the car?"

"I needed to do this."

He cupped her face in his hands and kissed her softly. Then not so softly. Slightly breathless she blinked at him when he lifted his head.

"Much better." He slicked his thumb over her bottom lip.

He surprised her by getting out of the car and walking around the hood. He opened her door and helped her out. She looked around and saw nothing but green rolling hills for miles.

"What are we doing?"

"Well, I'm going to be riding. And you are going to be driving."

"Really?" Squealing in excitement she threw herself into his arms. "Thank you. Thank you. Thank you." She peppered his face with kisses between each word.

"Wait." He caught her around the waist when she would have run for the driver's seat. "You do know how to drive a stick, right?"

"I do, yes." This time she pulled his head down to kiss him with all the love in her heart. She knew he was doing this to distract her from her funk, which made the gesture all the more special because he'd categorically refused to let her drive earlier. "I'll take care with your new baby."

He groaned but released her.

She practically danced her way to the driver's seat. Of course she had to have the roof down. That took all of fourteen seconds. Too cool. He took her through where everything was and she pushed the ignition.

Grinning, she said, "Put your seat belt on, lover."

And she put the car in gear.

Grave misgivings hounded Zach as he stared down at the crystal bauble in his hand. Two hearts entwined side by side. Christina's lucky brooch. He'd given up on finding it, given up on sabotaging the wedding, but he'd opened a small tapestry box in one of the trunks in Sophia's attic and there it was. Tarnished, with a few crystals missing, but unmistakable nonetheless.

He'd had no plan when he'd taken it, but for one bright moment he saw a light at the end of the tunnel of Tony's train-wreck plan to marry a woman he didn't love. Without the brooch might Christina back out of the wedding?

With no more thought than that he'd pocketed the trinket.

Now as he clutched it, he realized what he'd done. Christina wasn't backing out. Tony wasn't listening to Zach's appeals to rethink the madness. And Lindsay would freak if she ever learned he'd taken it. On every level professional, friends, lovers, she'd see it as a betrayal.

How could she not when that's what it felt like to him?

He wished he'd never seen it. Never taken it. Never risked everything he'd come to care so much about. Hell, he'd invested so much time in this wedding, even he cared about it being a success.

If only Tony wasn't the victim in all this.

It killed Zach to stand aside while his best friend set himself up for such a big fail. But there was no going back now. It didn't matter that the brooch was not wearable. Didn't matter that he had regrets. The damage was done.

He thought back to the conversation they'd had in the car on the way back from Sophia's. With the brooch burning a hole in his pocket he'd voiced his concerns for Tony and Lindsay had warned him interference never paid off.

"Do you know how many weddings there are where someone doesn't think it's a good idea for some reason?" she'd asked him. "The timing's not right, someone's too young, someone's too old, their ages are too far apart. They don't know what they're doing. She's all wrong for him. He's too good for her. Every one. Show me a wedding and there will be a dissenter in the crowd somewhere."

"They couldn't all be wrong."

"Oh, yeah. Some of them were spot-on. But has it ever worked out well when they try to intervene? No. Because it's not their decision to make. The heart wants what the heart wants."

"What if it isn't love?" he'd demanded.

"Then the situation that brought them together wants what it wants. If the couple is consenting adults, then it's their decision to make."

He heard the message. Understood that a marriage was between the man and woman involved. Still, it was hard to swallow when he knew this was a wedding that was never meant to be.

Glancing around, he looked for a place to stash the piece. Spying a likely spot, he buried it deep. After the wedding, he'd find a way to return the brooch to the Rose family.

In the meantime it was time he got on board and supported his friend.

* * *

"Hey," Lindsay called out to Zach where he still sat sipping coffee on the terrace. "I'm doing laundry today. I'm going to grab your stuff."

She went into his walk-in closet and gathered up the items in the hamper. There wasn't that much and she could easily handle it with her things. Something thumped to the floor as Zach filled the doorway.

A crystal brooch, two hearts entwined side-by-side, lay on the brown-and-rust rug.

Heart racing, she blinked once then again, hoping—no, praying—the view would change. Of course it didn't. Christina's brooch lay on the floor at her feet.

It had been hidden in Zach's dirty laundry. Because it was his dirty secret.

Pain bigger than anything she'd ever suffered tore through her heart.

"Lindsay." He stepped into the room that had seemed so big a moment ago but was now tiny and airless.

"You found the brooch." As if it might bite, she backed away from it. A heavy ball of dread lodged in her gut.

"Let me explain." He reached for her.

She pulled away from him.

"What's to explain? You kept it from me. Hid it." Rather than look at him, she stared down at the crystal pin. The silver was tarnished, a few crystals were missing; a beautiful piece ravished by time. It would need to be repaired before it could be worn again.

She lifted anguished eyes to his. "You lied to me."

"I didn't lie," he denied. "I just didn't reveal I'd found it."

"How is that not lying when our whole purpose for being there was to find the brooch?"

"You have to understand, I just want the two of them to stop and think about what they're doing. A lucky pin is a joke." He bent and picked it up. "This is a bandage at the best and a crutch at the very least."

"I understand perfectly." Her stomach roiled as nausea hit. She circled to the left, wanting out of the closet without touching him. "You haven't been helping me at all. You've been using your position as best man to spy on the wedding preparations. Oh, oh." As realization dawned, she retreated from him. When her back hit the wall she sank and wrapped her arms around her knees.

"It was your fault. I thought you were confessing because you felt bad. But it was your fault. You knew exactly what you were doing when you hired Fabio—or had a good idea, anyway. It was all you."

He went down on his haunches in front of her. She shrank away from him.

"Lindsay, this wasn't about you. You were never meant to get hurt."

She closed her eyes to block him out. "Go away."

"You have to listen to me."

"I can't believe anything you say."

"Antonio is a good guy. Always thinking of others. He's kept up with his duties while working in America. He's invested in a lot of businesses here, supported charities. Now he's giving up his life to be king, devoting his life to his country. He deserves to be happy. He has the right to choose his own wife."

"It's his life, Zach. He made his decision. He trusted you." She swallowed around the lump in her throat. "I trusted you."

"You don't understand" He rolled forward onto his knees. And still he loomed over her. "There's more at play here."

"I don't want to understand. I just want you to go away."

I can't." He sounded as if he had a mouth full of glass shards. "Not until I fix this."

"You can't fix this." She shook her head sadly. These past few days with him had been so perfect; a paradise of working and living together. Finding time to escape for a drive or some loving.

But it had been a fool's paradise.

"There's no undoing what's been done."

"There has to be." He reached for her.

She flinched from him.

His hand curled into a fist and fell to his side. "After the deal with the palazzo grounds I stopped.

I saw how upset you were and I couldn't be responsible for that. You were never meant to get hurt."

"Stop saying that. What did you expect to happen when a wedding I was planning fell apart at the seams?" How could he possibly believe she'd come out of the situation unscathed if the prince called off the wedding? She was right in the middle of it. Especially with all the little things that had gone wrong. Starting with him sitting on the wedding gown.

Oh, God.

Had he sat on the dress on purpose? Had he known even then who she was and planned to use her all along?

"No, of course not," he responded, revealing she'd spoken aloud. "I had this idea before I left home." He rubbed the back of his head in frustration. "I didn't know who you were when I boarded the plane. This wasn't about you. It was about saving Tony from a lifetime of misery. The wedding planner got paid either way. But I got the opportunity to save him."

Fury drove her to her feet. "You think I'm worried about getting paid? Damn you." She stormed from the closet, not stopping until she reached her room. Yanking her suitcase from where she'd stored it, she opened it on the bed and began dumping in clothes.

Of course he followed her. For such a smart man, he knew how to do stupid real well.

"Do you think I work for a paycheck? Is that all your work is to you? I bet not." She emptied the drawers into the case and went for her shoes. "I take pride in my work."

The shoes didn't fit. She forced herself to stop and fold. She would not come back here. She went into the bathroom and grabbed what toiletries she'd left down here. She clenched her teeth when she thought of the items now occupying space in the master bathroom. He could have them. No way was she going back in that room.

He still stood in the doorway when she returned to her room. His shoulders drooped and his features were haggard. He looked as though he'd lost something precious.

Good. He'd pulled her heart from her chest and stomped on it. Let him suffer.

"I take satisfaction in giving the bride and groom something special, a day they can look back on with pride and happiness."

She closed the suitcase, pushed on the lid a couple of times to mash it down and then started zipping.

"There's more involved than arranging the flowers and cuing the music." With her suitcase closed, she yanked it from the bed and pulled up the handle. Finally she lifted her chin and faced Zach. "But then, I know you don't put much value in what I do. I really should have listened when you said you hate big weddings."

"Lindsay, no—"

"What did you say?" She talked right over his

protest. "Oh, yeah, the couple needs to distract the crowd because they're marrying for something other than love."

"Don't do this. Don't leave. I didn't mean you."

"Oh, and let's not forget, love is a myth best left to romance novels."

He groaned.

"No, it's good this happened. Foolish me. I believed I was falling in love. It's so good to know it's just a myth. In a couple of days I'm sure I'll be fine."

She passed him in the doorway, making certain not to touch him. "But you should know there's nothing fake about what I do. I put my heart and soul into my weddings. And the couple doesn't walk away empty-handed. I make memories, Zach. I intend to give Antonio and Christina a spectacular wedding to look back on."

She turned her back on him and walked out. "Stay out of my way."

CHAPTER ELEVEN

AFTER SEVERAL DAYS of brooding, of waffling between righteous indignation and hating himself for the pain he'd caused Lindsay, Zach finally came to the conclusion the first was really no justification for the second.

She still used the sunroom as her workshop, but mostly Serena worked there and when Lindsay did come by, she kept the doors locked; a clear signal for him to stay out.

As he had for the past two evenings, he sat in the shadows of the patio, waiting to catch her when she left for the day. Hoping today she'd talk to him. He hadn't seen her at all yesterday and his chest ached with missing her.

In such a short time she'd burrowed her way into his affections. Watching her work fascinated him; the way she gathered a few odd items together and made something beautiful. Her expression when she concentrated was so fierce it was almost a scowl. Many times he'd wanted to run his thumb over the bow between her brows to see if her creative thoughts might transmit to him and show him what had her so enthralled.

He missed her wit, her laughter, the way she gave him a bad time.

Steps sounded on the spiral staircase and he surged to his feet, meeting her as she reached the patio level. The sun was setting behind her, casting her in a golden glow. Strands of her hair shimmered as a light breeze tossed them playfully around. In juxtaposition her blue eyes were guarded and the skin was pulled taut across her cheeks.

She made to walk by him and he caught her elbow in a light hold.

"Won't you talk to me for a minute?"

She didn't look at him. But she didn't pull away, either.

"There's nothing more to say between us."

"There is." He ran his thumb over the delicate skin of her inner elbow. Touching her fed something that had been deprived the past few days. Still, he forced himself to release her. "I tried to explain, but I failed to apologize. I'm sorry, Lindsay. I didn't think hard enough about how this would affect you. I never meant to devalue what you do."

Her shoulders squared and she half turned toward him. "But you don't value it. You've seen the effort involved, you can respect that. But you don't see the value in a beautiful wedding because you see it as the prelude to a flawed marriage."

"In this case, yes."

She sighed. "Zach, I've heard you talk about your parents enough to know what growing up with them must have been like. And I know you love Antonio, that he's probably closer to you than anyone. Mix that with your dislike of big, fancy weddings, and I'm sure this has been hell for you."

"I meant well," he avowed, grateful she saw what motivated him. "I can't stand the thought of him making this mistake, of him being miserable for the rest of his life. But Tony isn't rational when it comes to Halencia."

"Why? Because he refuses to see things your way?" She shook her head, the disappointment in her eyes almost harder to take than the hurt it replaced. "I think that's a good thing. I think a king should be willing to sacrifice for his country. Considering what his parents have put this country through, I think that's exactly what Halencia needs right now. And I think as his friend and best man, you should start showing him some support."

Hearing it broken down like that made him pause and rethink. Hadn't he had the same thought just days ago?

She took the opportunity to walk away. "I understand why you want to save Antonio. What I can't forgive is your willingness to sacrifice me to get it."

Unable to take anymore, Zack texted Tony.

Need to see you. I've messed up bad. You may want a new best man.

After sending the message, Tony wandered down to the pool to wait for the helicopter to arrive on the wide lawn they'd been using as a landing area. It would be at least an hour, but he had no desire to sit in the house so full of memories.

He stared at the pool and remembered the night he made love to Lindsay.

He couldn't regret it. Wouldn't.

Having her come alive in his arms was one of the high points in his life. He'd connected with her more closely than with any other woman he could recall. Her honest reactions and giving nature seduced him every bit as much as the silky feel of her skin and hair, the sweet taste of her mouth, the soft moans of her desire.

The few days he'd had her by his side had given him a brief glimpse into what the future could hold.

He wanted to scoff at the notion. To discount it as an indicator he'd been on one wild trip to Tuscany. But the truth was he could all too easily see her in his life. Not just here in Halencia but back in the States, as well.

And it scared the hell out of him.

The only thing that scared him more was the thought of losing her from his life altogether.

He knew the biggest betrayal for her was the intimacy they'd shared while she believed he'd been using her. But that's not what happened. He'd wanted Lindsay before he'd known she was the wedding planner. His attraction for her was completely disassociated from what she did.

Or so he'd thought.

Now he knew better. What she did was a part of who she was. She'd spoken of being disillusioned with her job. Her impassioned speech calling him to task for thinking a paycheck would suffice if the wedding fell apart proved she wasn't as lost as she'd feared. She'd been shaken because she let herself get caught up with Kevin and he'd used her.

It sickened Zach to realize he'd done the same thing.

Time to make it right.

The whoop, whoop, whoop of the helicopter sounded in the distance and grew louder. Finally. In another hour or so he'd see Tony, apologize for the mess he'd made of everything and put this whole fiasco behind him.

Being so close to Lindsay but parted from her drove him insane. He wanted to stay and fix it, but she needed to be here. He didn't. Hell, Tony probably wouldn't want him here when he learned what Zach had done.

He'd go back to the States and wait for her to come home. Then he'd find her and apologize again. No justifications, just a straight-up apology.

Ready to have this done, he strolled toward the helicopter. As he got closer he was surprised to see the pilot headed toward him. And then he knew.

"Tony." He broadened his stride and met his friend in a hug. "You came."

"Si, amico mio." Unselfconscious in showing emotion, Tony gave Zach a hard squeeze then stepped back to clap him on the arm. "Your text sounded serious."

"I've messed up."

"So you said. We must fix whatever you have done. I do not care to have anyone else for my best man."

"You haven't heard what I've done yet."

Tony had given up so much to support his country, would he be able to forgive Zach for messing in his affairs?

He couldn't lose both Lindsay and Antonio. Why hadn't he thought with his head instead of his heart?

"This sounds ominous." By mutual consent they headed toward the house. "You are my brother, Zach. You have seen how far I will go for my sibling. There is nothing you can do that will change my love for you. I need someone I can trust at my back during this wedding."

Zach walked at his friend's side. They were passing near the pool when Tony stopped. He looked longingly at the pool.

"Ah, the water looks good. I have not been swimming since I got to Halencia."

"You want to swim?" Zach grabbed his shirt at the back of the neck and pulled it off over his head. "It's as good a place to talk as any."

He stripped down and dove in. As soon as the water embraced him, he struck out, arm overhead, legs kicking, arm overhead, kick, again and again. He needed the physical exertion to empty his mind of everything but the tracking of laps and the knowledge Tony matched him pace for pace.

Tony tapped his shoulder when they reached fifty. "Let's hit the spa."

Zach slicked a hand over his face and hair and nodded.

In one big surge, he propelled himself up and out of the pool. He walked to the controls for the spa and flicked the switch to generate the jets. After grabbing a couple of towels from a storage ottoman and tossing them on the end of a lounger near the spa, he hit the mini fridge for a couple sodas and joined his friend, sighing as the hot water engulfed him.

"*Grazie.*" Tony took a big swig and closed his blue eyes on a groan as he let his head fall back. "You don't know how good this feels. Hey, I know you're working with the palace liaison on the bachelor party but can we do it here? Keep it tight and quiet."

"Sure. How about poker, cigars and a nice, aged whiskey?"

"Perfect." Tony laughed. "Now, tell me what's up."

Zach did, he laid it all out, not bothering to spare himself. "The good news is you'll still have a beautiful wedding, but I think I should go."

"It's not like you to run, Zach."

He barked a harsh laugh. "None of this is like me."

"True. You actually let her drive your new car?"

Zach eyed his friend still laying back and letting the jets pound him with bubbles. "Focus, dude. I almost wrecked your wedding."

"But you didn't." Tony straightened and spread his arms along the edge of the spa. He nailed Zach with an intent stare. "You messed up your life instead. You care about Ms. Reeves."

He got a little sick every time he thought about never seeing her again. But that wasn't something he was willing to share.

"She's a good person. And she's really worked hard to give you and Christina an event to be proud of. She found these cool candleholders that merge your two styles—"

"Stop." Tony held up a dripping hand. "I'm going

to stop you right there. Dude, you're spouting wedding drivel. Obviously you're in love."

"Shut up." Zach cursed and threw his empty soda can at his friend's head. "You know I don't do love."

"I know you have a big heart or you wouldn't care so much about my future. You deserve to be happy, my friend, and I think the wedding planner makes you happy."

How easily Tony read him. Zach had been happier here in Halencia than as far back as he could remember. But he'd ruined any chance of finishing the trip in the same vein.

"You deserve happiness, too. That's all I really wanted when I started this mess."

"I appreciate that you want me to be happy. But this is something I have to do. To be honest, the thought of a love match would terrify me. Watching the roller coaster that has been my parents' marriage cured me of that. I will be happy to have a peaceful arrangement with a woman I can admire and respect who will stand by my side and represent my country. Like your Lindsay, Christina is a good woman. We will find our way. You need to do the same."

His Lindsay. That sounded good.

"My being here hurts her. It's best if I leave and let her do her job."

"You mean it's easier. Well, forget it. You're my

best man and I'm not letting you off the hook. Relationships take work, Zach."

That's what Lindsay said when she was talking about her mother's many marriages.

"If you care for this woman, and it appears you do, you need to fight for her. Apologize."

"I did. She didn't want to hear it."

Tony cocked a sardonic eyebrow. "Apologize again."

Zach nodded. "Right."

"Tell her you love her."

Love. Zach held his friend's gaze for a long moment, letting unfamiliar emotions—confusion, fear, sadness, exhilaration, joy, hope—rush through him. And finally he nodded. "Right."

A knock sounded at Lindsay's door. She ignored it. Now she was back at the hotel she was fair game for the press who thought nothing about knocking on her door at all hours. So pushy.

Another bang on the door.

She kept her attention on her schedule for the next week. Circled in red at the end of the week was *the* day. The wedding.

The rehearsal was in two days, four days in advance of the actual event because it was the only day everyone could get together. She'd have to see Zach, deal with him. As long as he didn't start apologizing again, she'd be fine.

She knew he'd meant well, that he loved Antonio like a brother. She even admired how far he was willing to go to ensure his friend's happiness.

But she couldn't tolerate the fact that she was acceptable collateral damage.

Why did men find her so dispensable?

She was fairly smart, had a good sense of humor. She worked hard; if anything, too hard. She was honest, kind, punctual. Okay, she wasn't model beautiful, but she wasn't hideous, either.

So what made her so unlovable?

More knocking. Ugh, these guys were relentless.

"Signorina? Signorina?" Mario called out. "Are you there? Mama says you should come."

Oh, gosh. She'd left the poor kid standing out there. Lindsay set her tablet aside and rushed to the door.

"Signorina." Mario greeted her anxiously. "Someone is here to see you. Mama says you must come."

Lindsay gritted her teeth. Zach. Why couldn't he leave her be? "Can you tell him I'm busy?"

His eyes grew big and he frantically shook his head. "No, *signorina*. You must come."

She'd never seen the boy so agitated. Fine, she'd just go tell Zach, once more, to leave her alone. Mario led her downstairs to a room she hadn't seen before. A man stood looking out on the rose garden.

"Zach you need to stop— Oh, sorry." She came

to an abrupt halt when the man turned. Not Zach. "Oh, goodness. Prince Antonio. Your Highness."

Should she curtsy? Why hadn't she practiced curtsying?

"Ms. Reeves, thank you for seeing me." He spoke in slightly accented English and had the bluest eyes she'd ever seen. They twinkled as he took her hand and bowed over it in a gesture only the European did well. "I hope you are not thinking of curtsying. It is entirely unnecessary."

His charm and humor put her instantly at ease. That ability, along with his dark, good looks and the sharp intelligence in those incredible eyes, would serve him well as King of Halencia. She wondered if they'd approached him about running for president.

"You're here to plead his case, aren't you?" Why else would the prince seek her out? He'd showed little to no interest in the wedding plans, even through his advocate.

Anger heated her blood. How dare Zach put her in this position? What could the prince think but that she allowed her personal business to interfere with his wedding preparations? Showing no interest and having none were two different things.

This whole situation just got worse and worse.

"I am." Prince Antonio indicated she should sit.

She perched on the edge of a beige sofa. The prince sat adjacent to her in a matching recliner.

"Your Highness, I can assure you the plans for

the wedding are on schedule. And, of course, I will continue to work with Zach as your representative, but anything beyond working together is over. He should not have involved you."

"Please, call me Tony."

Yeah, that wasn't going to happen.

"You are obviously important to Zach and he is important to me, so we should be friendly, *si*?"

She meant to nod; a silent, polite gesture to indicate she heard him. But her head shook back and forth, the denial too instinctive.

"He does not know I am here."

That got her attention. "He didn't send you?"

"No. In fact he planned to leave Halencia, to concede the field to you, as it were. He wanted to make it easier on you."

"Oh." What did she make of that? He was supposed to be best man. Of course he'd have to tell the prince if he planned to leave. Had he already left? Was that why Antonio was here, to tell her she'd be working with a new best man?

Her heart clenched at the thought of never seeing Zach again. The sense of loss cut through the anger and hurt like a sword through butter.

"But he is my best friend. I do not want another for my best man."

"Oh." Huge relief lifted the word up. The feeling of being reprieved was totally inappropriate. He'd used and betrayed her. That hadn't changed. Just as her foolish love for him hadn't changed. It was those softer feelings that tried to sway her now.

Too bad she'd learned she couldn't trust those feelings.

"I have never seen Zach so enamored of a woman. Is it true he let you drive his car?"

She nodded. And she knew why. In piecing things together she figured that must be the trip where Zach had found the pin. She'd been brooding on the trip back and he'd felt guilty.

As he should.

The prince laughed, drawing her attention.

"He really does have it bad. I wish I could have been here to watch this courtship."

"There's been no courtship, Your Highness. Far from it." She'd stayed strong for two weeks. Why, oh, why had she let his vulnerability get to her? Because she'd fallen for him. Her mom was fond of saying you couldn't control who you fell in love with. Lindsay always considered that a tad convenient.

Turned out it wasn't convenient at all.

"Antonio," he insisted. "I am hoping I can persuade you to cut him some slack. I am quite annoyed with him myself, but I understand what drove him. Zach is not used to having people in his life that matter to him. He is a numbers man. He would have calculated the risk factors and figured those associated with you were tolerable. If the wedding was called off, you would still get paid."

"So he said, but there's more than a paycheck involved here. There's my reputation, as well."

"Which would not suffer if I or Christina called off the wedding."

"It would if it was due to a jinxed wedding, which I can only speculate is what he hoped to achieve."

"Was it such a bad thing he did? Fighting for my happiness?"

"That's not fair." She chided him with her gaze but had to look away as tears welled. She had to clear her throat before speaking. "People don't use the people that matter to them."

Something close to sadness came and went in his blue eyes. "Yes, we do. We are just more up front about it. Zach told me you have the brooch."

It took a second for her brain to switch gears "Yes. It's in my room. It's damaged so I haven't mentioned we found it to Christina yet."

"This is good. If you please, I'd like to take it with me to see if I can get it repaired in time for the wedding."

"Of course. I'll go get it." She quickly made the trip to her room and returned to hand him the antique piece. "It's really a lovely design."

"Yes, two hearts entwined side by side." Expression thoughtful, he ran his thumb over the crystals.

"You can see why it represents true love and longevity."

"Indeed. I hope you are able to get it repaired in time. More, I hope it brings you and Christina much happiness."

"*Grazie*, Ms. Reeves. I can see why Zach has fallen for you. I think you will be good for him."

She sighed on a helpless shrug. "Your Highness."

"Antonio." He bent and kissed her cheek. "As you think about his sins, I wish for you to consider something, as well."

Cautious, she asked, "What's that?"

"Zach does not let anyone drive his cars."

She opened her mouth on a protest.

He stopped her with a raised hand. "Not even me."

She blinked at him as his words sank in, biting her tongue to hold back another ineffective "Oh."

He nodded. "Zach told you of Julia?"

She inclined her head in acknowledgment.

"Ah. Another sign of his affection for you. He does not talk about himself easily. He does not speak of Julia at all. He thought he should have known, that he should have seen through her avarice to her true motives. He's never been as open or as giving since. Until now."

Antonio stepped to the door. "Please do not tell Christina of the brooch. I do not want her to be disappointed if it is not ready in time." With a bow of his head, he took his leave.

Lindsay continued to look at where he'd been. She wrapped her arms around herself, needing to hold on to something. Because everything she believed had just been shaken up.

The Prince of Halencia had come to see her, to plead Zach's case after he'd tried to sabotage Antonio's wedding. How mixed up was that? If Antonio could overlook Zach's craziness, could—should—Lindsay?

Hurt and anger gripped her in unrelenting talons, digging deep, tearing holes in her soul. She wanted to think this would let up after a couple of weeks of nursing the hurt as it had with Kevin, but this went deeper, stung harder.

What she felt for Kevin had been make-believe; more in her head than anything else. What she felt for Zach came from the heart. And it hadn't stopped just because he'd hurt her. The wrenching sickness in her gut when Antonio'd said Zach planned to leave proved that.

Seeking fresh air, she slipped out of the house and into the dark garden. Lights from the house showed her the way to a path that led to the back of the garden where a bench sat beside a tinkling fountain.

The earthy scent of imminent rain hung in the air. Lindsay looked up. No stars confirmed clouds were overhead.

Great. A storm. Just what she needed.

But it wasn't fear or an uneasiness that took control of her head. Memories of being stuck in Zach's car and staying with him at the farmhouse B and B in Caprese bombarded her.

He'd held her, a stranger, because she was afraid. He'd listened to her sad tale of being scared because her mother always cried during storms. The truth was her father left during a storm and deep down in her child's psyche, she'd feared her mother would leave, too, and Lindsay would be all alone.

Antonio had asked if Zach's fighting for his happiness was such a bad thing.

And the answer was no. She understood Zach's motivation. He'd grown up a victim of his parents' political alliance and the trip to see them en route to Halencia probably trigged the need to intervene on Antonio's behalf.

If this were just the summer fling she'd convinced herself she could handle, she'd forgive him and move on.

But she loved him.

She dipped her fingers in the fountain and swirled the water around. It was still warm from the heat of the day.

She missed the villa. Missed sharing coffee with Zach in the morning seated out on the terrace watching the city come alive down below. She missed his sharp mind and dry humor and his total ignorance of all things wedding-related.

But most of all she missed the way he held her, as if she were the most precious thing in his world.

And that's what she couldn't forgive.

He'd made her believe she mattered. And it had all been a lie.

She'd never been put first before.

Her dad had walked out before she even knew him. And her mother loved her. But Lindsay had always known her mother's wants and needs came first. Even when it was just Lindsay, work came first.

For a few magical days Zach had made her feel as if she was his everything. It showed in the way he'd touched her and by the heat in his eyes. It was in the deference and care he'd demonstrated, the affection and tenderness.

Maybe it was a facade he assumed and that's how he treated all the women in his life—the thought sliced through her brain like shards of broken glass—but it felt real to her. And she couldn't—wouldn't—accept less just to finish out a summer fling.

No more settling. She'd done that with Kevin and learned her lesson. She'd been willing to settle for a fling with Zach because she'd sensed how good it would be between them. And she'd been right. But she loved him, and a fling was no longer enough.

She needed honesty, respect and a willingness to put your partner first.

How often had she watched her mother's relationships fall apart because a little work was involved? Her mom was so used to being the center of her world she didn't see that sometimes she needed to make her husband feel he was the center of her world.

Antonio inferred Zach cared for her. He made it sound as if Zach had planned to leave to make things easier for her. More likely he'd wanted out of this whole gig. But there was the bit about letting her drive his car when he never let anyone drive his cars, not even the man he thought of as his brother.

No. Just stop. She pushed the wistful thinking aside as she headed inside. His actions told the story. He didn't love her. He'd proved that when he'd put his friend before her.

Zach had said he liked storms, for him they washed things clean, made them shiny and new, allowing new growth. A good metaphor for him. He was the storm that allowed her to put the horror of Kevin's betrayal behind her. But would her heart survived the tsunami Zach had left in his wake?

CHAPTER TWELVE

TWO DAYS LATER Lindsay walked with Serena toward
the Palazzo di Comparino chapel. The rehearsal
started in twenty minutes. Nothing was going right
today. She should be totally focused on damage control and all she could think about was the fact she'd
be seeing Zach in a few minutes.

Her mind and heart played a mad game of table
tennis over him. One moment she was strong and
resolute in holding out for what she deserved. The
next she was sure she deserved him, that his actions
proved he cared deeply for the people in his life and
she wanted to be one of those people.

"You just got an email from Christina confirming she will not make it to the rehearsal." Serena
jogged to keep up.

Lindsay came to a full stop, causing Serena to
backtrack. "What about Antonio?"

"He is still delayed at the palace, but he is trying to get here."

"Okay, we're talking a good two hours. Let me

call Raffaele to see if he can move dinner up." Before the big blowup between them, she'd suggested to Zach that he host the rehearsal dinner at the villa. With her taking care of the details, he'd been happy to agree.

It was a no-brainer to put Mancini's in charge of the food. Still moving dinner up an hour would be a challenge. But so worth it if it allowed if at least one of the bridal couple to make it to the rehearsal.

"The prince's email said we should start without him."

"Wonderful. Zach will have to act as the groom and can you play the part of Christina?"

"Oh, Lindsay, I am sorry, but I cannot."

"Sure you can. I know these are high-profile people, but all you have to do is walk slowly down the aisle. No biggie."

"No, remember, Papa and I are meeting the glass-blower to pick up the last delivery of candleholders. I have to leave in half an hour."

"Oh, yeah, that's tonight. Well, of course. Why should anything workout tonight?"

"Perhaps Papa can go on his own?" Serena made the offer hesitantly. Generous of her since Lindsay knew the two were looking forward to the road trip. A little father-daughter time before Serena went back to school.

"No, you go. I know this trip means a lot to you. I'll work something out."

"You could play the bride," Serena suggested.

"Uh, no. Thanks, but I have to keep things moving." So not a good idea. The very notion of walking down the aisle to Zach in groom mode messed with her head.

And her heart.

The elderly priest had other ideas. He looked like a monk of days gone by and he held her hand and patted the back ever so gently. He spoke softly, listened carefully, and totally took over the rehearsal. Everything must be just so.

He explained what was going to happen, who was going to go where, who stood, who sat, who would leave first and who would follow. He was quite thorough.

Because she found her gaze repeatedly finding Zach, who looked gorgeous in a white shirt and dark sports jacket, Lindsay ran her gaze over the participants. Everyone listened respectfully. Even Queen Valentina and the king, who sat holding hands. Apparently they were in an "on again" phase of their relationship.

The chapel looked lovely. A rainbow of colors fell through the stained-glass windows and standing candleholders in white wrought-iron lined the walls from the back to the front and across the altar, illuminating the small interior. For the wedding they would be connected with garlands of sunflowers and roses.

And from what she observed, the palace photographer seemed to be doing a good job. He was the only extra person in the room. Serena had quietly made her departure during the priest's soliloquy.

"Come, come." The priest raised his cupped hands as if lifting a baby high. "Let us all take our places. You, young man—" he patted Zach on the shoulder "—will play the part of the groom. And you, *signorina*—" he looked at Lindsay "—will be our bride today."

No, no, no.

Pasting on a serene smile, she politely refused. "I'm sorry, Father, I really need to observe and take notes to ensure a smooth ceremony the day of the wedding."

"*Si, si.* You will observe as the bride. Come, stand here." He motioned to his right.

Zach stood tall and broad on the priest's left.

She swallowed hard and shook her head. She couldn't do it. She couldn't pretend to be Zach's bride when she longed for the truth of the position with all her broken heart.

"Perhaps Elena can play the bride?" she suggested. Hoped.

"Oh, no. Elena has her own role to play as the maid of honor. You are needed, *signorina*. Come."

There was no protesting after that. Plus, others would begin to make note if she made any more of a scene. Clenching her teeth together, she moved forward, holding her tablet in front of her like a shield, looking everywhere but at Zach.

She was fine while the priest directed the action from the altar, but when he stepped away to help people find their spots, Zach narrowed the distance between them by a step then two.

"Please don't start anything here," she implored.

"I'm not." He put his hands in his pockets and rocked on his heels. "How have you been?"

"We should listen to the Father."

"I've missed you."

"Zach, I can't do this here."

"You have to give me something, Lindsay. You asked me to stay away and I have."

She narrowed her eyes at him. "You've texted me several times every day." Crazy things, thoughtful things, odd facts about himself. She'd wanted to delete them without reading them, but she'd read every one, came to look forward to them, especially those that revealed something about him.

"I needed some link to you. I'm afraid I'm addicted."

"You're not going to charm me, Zach." She frantically searched out the priest. When was this show going to get on the road? When she looked back, Zach was closer still.

He bent over her. "You smell so good. Do you miss me at all?"

"Every minute of every day." Her hand went to her mouth. Oh, my dog. Did she just say that out loud?

"Lindsay—"

"The priest is calling me." Heart racing, she escaped to the back of the chapel where the wedding party congregated. The priest nodded when she appeared, as if he'd been waiting for her.

"*Si, si*. We will start with the procession. Just as I described. *Signorina*, you will be last with Signor Rose."

Lindsay took her place by the robust man who made no effort to disguise his disapproval of Christina's absence. She wasn't Lindsay's favorite person at the moment, either.

Oh, gosh, instead of settling, her heart raced harder. Zach stood at the altar waiting for her to come to him. It felt too real. And, sweet merciful heavens, she wished it were real.

It mattered what he'd done. Yes, he'd meant well. And no, he hadn't known her when he initiated his plan. But it mattered.

The procession began to move. She closed her eyes and stepped forward. Her foot slipped on the uneven ground, so, okay, that wasn't going to work. She opened her eyes and concentrated on the smooth stones of the chapel floor.

He had apologized. And he'd honored her request to stay away. But he hadn't let her forget him, or the time they'd spent together.

Had that been him fighting for her? Or was that wishful thinking?

Suddenly, Mr. Rose stopped and Zach's strong, tanned hand came into view. She fought the urge to put her hands behind her back. All eyes were on her, on them, but this was for Antonio and Christina's wedding. Nobody cared about her or Zach; they didn't care that touching him would be a huge mistake.

She hated how her hand shook as she placed it in his.

He set her hand on his arm and led her to stand in front of the priest. And then he covered her hand with his warm hold and leaned close to whisper, "No need to be nervous. I'm right here by your side."

For some odd reason she actually found his promise reassuring. Facing the priest, not so much.

"Well done, well done." He motioned for the wedding party to be seated. "Lindsay, Zach, if you will face each other. Next I will begin the ceremony. I'll share a few words and then we'll go through the exit procession."

Lindsay turned to face Zach and he took both her hands in each of his. It was the most surreal moment of her life.

The priest began. "Today is a glorious day which the Lord hath made, as today both of you are blessed with God's greatest of all gifts, the gift of abiding love and devotion between a man and woman. All present here today, and those here in heart, wish both of you all the joy, happiness and success the world has to offer—"

"Stop. I can't do this." Lindsay tried to pull away. This hurt too much.

"Lindsay, it's okay." Zach's voice was calm and steady. His hold remained sure and strong as he moved to shield her from the audience. "Father, may we have a moment?"

"Of course, my son." The priest bowed and moved away.

"Breathe, Lindsay. It's going to be okay." Zach leaned over her. "I felt it, too. How right those words were between you and me."

Lindsay clutched at Zach's hands, clinging to him as emotions raged through her heart and head.

"I can't do this. I'm sorry." Aware her behavior embarrassed both her and him, she lifted bleak eyes to meet his gaze. What she saw made the breath catch in her throat.

His eyes were unshielded and in the dark, whiskey depths shone a love so big and so deep it seemed to go on forever. She felt surrounded in a cushion of caring, lifted on a throne of adoration.

"Zach," she breathed.

"I love you, Lindsay." The words echoed everything his eyes already revealed.

Hope slowly swelled through her as her love

surged to the surface eager for all his gaze offered. Already weakened, her self-preservation instincts began to crumble as unleashed longing filled her heart.

"I hurt you and I'm more sorry than I can say that I let the fears of my childhood control my common sense when it came to Tony's wedding. You opened my eyes to what I was doing and he hammered it home. But even when I finally accepted the truth and apologized, something still nagged at me, a sense of wrongness that grew rather than diminished."

Behind him she was aware of movement and whispers, reminding her they were not alone. But all she heard, all she saw, was Zach and the raw pain filling eyes that had been overflowing with love just moments ago.

"And then the truth came to me. I couldn't get past how my actions hurt you. I wronged you, not just by disrespecting what you do and by making you work harder, but by putting Tony's needs before yours. That's when I knew the happiness I take in your company and the joy that consumes me when I touch you is actually love."

Now his hands were tight on hers. She ran her thumbs softly over the whites of his knuckles. Everything he'd said was just what she'd longed to hear. She let the last of her concerns melt away.

"Zach." She squeezed his hands. "I love you, too."

Relief flooded his features and he rested his forehead against hers. "Thank God. Because this is bigger and more terrifying than anything I've ever known."

A laugh trilled out of her. "Yes. I'm glad to know I'm not alone."

"You'll never be alone again." He raised his head and his love rained down on her. "Watching you walk down that aisle to me felt more right than anything else in my life. I love you, Lindsay Reeves. Will you marry me?"

"Yes." No hesitation, no need to think. Her misery had come from that same sense of rightness. She longed to spend the rest of her life with this man. "I would love to marry you."

"Right now?" His brown gaze danced with love and mischief.

She blinked at him. "What?"

"Will you marry me right now, in this beautiful chapel we refashioned together?"

Her mind slowly grasped what he wanted, and then her heart soared with excited anticipation. Still, she couldn't get married without her mother. "What about our friends and family?"

"We can have a lavish ceremony back in the States. As big as you want. But I don't want to wait to claim you as mine. So I made sure everyone who truly matters is here."

He stepped back to reveal the chapel filled with

people. She saw Louisa sandwiched between Nico and Vincenzo. Raffaele and Daniella sat next to Eva and Mario. Alonso and Serena were here instead of on the road. And many more of the townspeople she'd met and worked with over the past month filled the pews, including the King and Queen of Halencia.

And standing with the grinning priest was Prince Antonio and…her mother.

"Mom?"

"I knew you'd want her here." Zach's hand rested warm and familiar in the small of her back.

"You must have been planning this for days."

"It's the only thing that's kept me sane." He lifted her chin, his mouth settling on hers in restrained urgency. When he raised his head, his eyes gleamed with the heat of desire, the steadfastness of love. "Shall we do this?"

She nodded slowly. "Yes."

Her answer ignited a flurry of activity. Antonio stepped forward while her mother grabbed her hand and hustled her back down the aisle and out the door. In an instant she was in her mom's arms being hugged hard.

"I'm so happy for you, baby. Zach is a force of nature. If he loves you anywhere near as much as his actions indicate, you will have a long and joyous marriage." She sighed. "For all my marriages, I've never had anyone look at me with so much love."

Lindsay was too excited to have her mother here to care that her special day had circled around to focus on her mom's feelings.

"I'm so glad you're here. You look beautiful." Her mom wore a lovely, pale green silk suit that went well with her upswept brown hair and green eyes. "And you're wrong. Matt looks at you like that. You've just been too focused on yourself to notice."

"Lindsay!" her mother protested, but a speculative glint entered her eyes. "I'll let that slide. We need to get you ready."

"I think I'm as ready as we have time for." Lindsay glanced down at her flowing ivory dress that came to just below her knees in the front and to her ankles in the back and knew she'd been set up. Serena had insisted the dress was perfect for today; business moving into party mode. Of everything she owned this would have been her choice for an impromptu wedding gown.

"Oh, we have time for a few special touches." Darlene pulled Lindsay around the side of the chapel where a full-length, gold-framed mirror leaned against the side of the building, next to it was a garment rack with a flow of tulle over one end and a stack of shelves hanging from the other.

"Something old." From the shelves her mother lifted out a set of pearl-and-sapphire earrings.

"Grandma's earrings." Darlene had worn them for her first wedding and Lindsay recalled saying wistfully she'd wear them at her wedding someday. Her mother had remembered. Her hands shook a little as she put them on.

"Something new." A beaded belt and matching shoes adorned in pearls and crystals shimmered in the late-afternoon sun. While Lindsay traded her sandals for the high-heeled pumps, Darlene stepped behind her and clipped it into place at her waist. They both fit perfectly.

"Something borrowed." Mom smiled. "I saved this because you loved it so much." The tulle turned out to be a full-length veil scalloped on the edges in delicate pearl-infused embroidery. "Close your eyes and face the mirror."

Lindsay's heart expanded; she hadn't realized her mother had been paying such close attention to her reactions through the years. She closed her eyes against a well of tears while Darlene fussed with the veil and the lovely floral hair clip that went with it.

Next she felt a rouge brush dust over her cheeks and some gloss being dabbed on her lips. A tissue caught an escaping tear.

"You can open your eyes."

Lindsay did and was amazed to find a beautiful bride staring back at her. "Mom."

"You're stunning, baby."

Lindsay nodded. She felt stunning and ready to begin her life with Zach.

"Let's go. Your man is waiting."

Rounding the corner of the chapel, she spied the replica of the fountain from the plaza and thought of the wish she'd made with Zach. The wish for true love had been meant for Antonio and Christina. Lindsay supposed she'd been pushing it to make a wish for another couple, but she couldn't be disappointed that fate had chosen to grant true love to her and Zach.

This time when she walked down the aisle her mother escorted her and Lindsay's heart swelled with joy as her gaze locked with Zach's. He'd changed into the suit he'd been wearing when they'd met and she loved the symbolism of the gesture. He knew her so well.

There was no shaking as she placed her hand in his, just a surety of purpose, a promise to always be there for him. The warmth and steadiness of his grip was the same as it had been earlier and she recognized he'd always be her rock. She suddenly realized something she'd missed when taking in the surprise he'd given her.

"What about your parents?" she whispered.

"They couldn't make it."

"I'm sorry." And angry. His parents didn't deserve him.

"Pixie—" he cupped her cheek "—you're all the family I need."

Her throat closed on a swell of emotion. She swallowed and pledged. "I love you."

"I can't wait for you to be my wife."

"Ahem." Antonio placed his hand on Zach's shoulder. "The priest is waiting."

"Right." Love and anticipation bright in his gaze, he gave the nod. "We're ready, Father."

"We are gathered together on this glorious day which the Lord hath made, to witness the joining of Zachary Sullivan and Lindsay Reeves, who have been blessed with God's greatest of all gifts, the gift of abiding love and devotion between a man and woman…"

* * * * *

COMING NEXT MONTH FROM

HARLEQUIN

Romance

Available January 5, 2016

#4503 HIS PRINCESS OF CONVENIENCE
The Vineyards of Calanetti
by Rebecca Winters

Christina Rose longs for a fairy-tale wedding, but her betrothal to Prince Antonio was a ruse—they weren't supposed to actually marry! As the wedding bells begin to ring, dare she hope Antonio says "I love you" as well as "I do"...?

#4504 HOLIDAY WITH THE MILLIONAIRE
Tycoons in a Million
by Scarlet Wilson

Lara has never been lucky in love and is in need of a holiday...she just never expected it to be with millionaire Reuben. As they travel the world together, Reuben makes Lara feel beautiful again, but can she show the playboy that he too is worthy of love?

#4505 THE HUSBAND SHE'D NEVER MET
by Barbara Hannay

After waking up from an accident, Carrie finds a ring on her finger and a husband by her side—if only she could remember him! But tycoon Max is determined to help Carrie rediscover all the reasons they fell in love, by recreating their romance, one magical date at a time...

#4506 UNLOCKING HER BOSS'S HEART
by Christy McKellen

Max Firebrace doesn't think he'll ever love again, but when his new PA, beautiful and brave Cara Winstone, walks into his life, this brooding boss begins to wonder if he's ready for a new happy-ever-after...with Cara by his side!

HRLPCNM1215

LARGER-PRINT BOOKS!
GET 2 FREE LARGER-PRINT NOVELS PLUS
2 FREE GIFTS!

HARLEQUIN

Romance

From the Heart, For the Heart

YES! Please send me 2 FREE LARGER-PRINT Harlequin® Romance novels and my 2 FREE gifts (gifts are worth about $10). After receiving them, if I don't wish to receive any more books, I can return the shipping statement marked "cancel." If I don't cancel, I will receive 4 brand-new novels every month and be billed just $5.09 per book in the U.S. or $5.49 per book in Canada. That's a savings of at least 15% off the cover price! It's quite a bargain! Shipping and handling is just 50¢ per book in the U.S. and 75¢ per book in Canada.* I understand that accepting the 2 free books and gifts places me under no obligation to buy anything. I can always return a shipment and cancel at any time. Even if I never buy another book, the two free books and gifts are mine to keep forever.

119/319 HDN GHWC

Name	(PLEASE PRINT)

Address	Apt. #

City	State/Prov.	Zip/Postal Code

Signature (if under 18, a parent or guardian must sign)

Mail to the **Reader Service:**
IN U.S.A.: P.O. Box 1867, Buffalo, NY 14240-1867
IN CANADA: P.O. Box 609, Fort Erie, Ontario L2A 5X3
Want to try two free books from another line?
Call 1-800-873-8635 or visit www.ReaderService.com.

* Terms and prices subject to change without notice. Prices do not include applicable taxes. Sales tax applicable in N.Y. Canadian residents will be charged applicable taxes. Offer not valid in Quebec. This offer is limited to one order per household. Not valid for current subscribers to Harlequin Romance Larger-Print books. All orders subject to credit approval. Credit or debit balances in a customer's account(s) may be offset by any other outstanding balance owed by or to the customer. Please allow 4 to 6 weeks for delivery. Offer available while quantities last.

Your Privacy—The Reader Service is committed to protecting your privacy. Our Privacy Policy is available online at www.ReaderService.com or upon request from the Reader Service.

We make a portion of our mailing list available to reputable third parties that offer products we believe may interest you. If you prefer that we not exchange your name with third parties, or if you wish to clarify or modify your communication preferences, please visit us at www.ReaderService.com/consumerschoice or write to us at Reader Service Preference Service, P.O. Box 9062, Buffalo, NY 14240-9062. Include your complete name and address.

HRLP15

SPECIAL EXCERPT FROM

◆ HARLEQUIN®
™

Romance

*As the wedding bells begin to ring, will Prince Antonio
say "I love you" as well as "I do"…?*

*Read on for a sneak preview of
HIS PRINCESS OF CONVENIENCE,
the penultimate book in the breathtaking
THE VINEYARDS OF CALANETTI*

Once again they hiked up the side to the top. Before they went out on the rocks he plucked a white flower with a gardenia scent, growing on a nearby vine. He tucked it behind her ear. "Now you're my Polynesian princess."

Her eyes wandered over him. "I don't ever want to go home."

"Then we won't." He grabbed her hand and they inched their way onto the rocks until the force of the water took them over the edge. It was like free-falling into space until the water caught them and brought them to the surface.

Together they swam to the edge of the pool where they'd left their packs. He helped her out of the water and they proceeded to set up camp. After they'd made their bed, they put out the food. The exertion had made them hungry. They sat across from each other and ate to their hearts' content. He finally stretched.

"I've never felt so good, never tasted food so good, never been with anyone I enjoyed more. In truth, I've never been this happy in my life."

"I feel the same way," she responded. "I want it to last, but I know it's not going to."

He shook his head. "Shh. Don't spoil this heavenly evening. We have two more days and nights ahead of us."

"You're right."

"You've lost your gardenia. I'm going to pick another one."

When he returned, he hunkered down next to her and put it behind her ear. "This is how I'm always going to remember you."

Antonio couldn't wait to get close to her again and cleaned up their picnic. When everything had been put away, she started to leave but he caught her by the ankle. "Stay with me."

"I was just going to get out of my bathing suit."

"But I want to hold you first." He pulled her down and rolled on his side so he could look at her. "I've been waiting all day for tonight to come."

"So have I." Her voice throbbed.

He pulled her into him and claimed her luscious mouth that had given him a heart attack last night. "You could have no idea how much I want you. Love me, Christina. I need you."

Don't miss
HIS PRINCESS OF CONVENIENCE
by Rebecca Winters,
available January 2016 wherever
Harlequin® Romance books and ebooks are sold.

www.Harlequin.com